BETTER HOMES AND GUARDENS

Publisher **MIKE RICHARDSON**
Senior Editor **PHILIP R. SIMON**
Assistant Editor **JOSHUA ENGLEDOW**
Designer **BRENNAN THOME**
Digital Art Technician **ALLYSON HALLER**

Special thanks to Joshua Franks, Julie Kim, Jessica Leung, A.J. Rathbun, Kristen Star, and everyone at PopCap Games and EA Games.

First Edition: February 2020
ISBN 978-1-50671-305-2

10 9 8 7 6 5 4 3 2 1
Printed in China

DarkHorse.com
PopCap.com

No plants were harmed in the making of this graphic novel. However, many editors purchased Guard-en plants from Crazy Dave, and a few of us traded with him. (Don't ask.) We've mounted Guard-ens to our beloved office therapy dogs, who now patrol our mostly-zombie-free offices! Now, if we could only schedule a Zombie Alert Siren installation . . .

PLANTS vs. ZOMBIES: BETTER HOMES AND GUARDENS | Published by Dark Horse Books, a division of Dark Horse Comics LLC, 10956 SE Main Street, Milwaukie, OR 97222 | To find a comics shop in your area, visit comicshoplocator.com |

Library of Congress Cataloging-in-Publication Data

Names: Tobin, Paul, 1965- writer. | Gillenardo-Goudreau, Christianne, artist. | Breckel, Heather, colourist. | Dutro, Steve, letterer.
Title: Better homes and guardens / written by Paul Tobin ; art by Christianne Gillenardo-Goudreau ; colors by Heather Breckel ; letters by Steve Dutro ; cover by Christianne Gillenardo-Goudreau.
Description: First edition. | Milwaukie, OR : Dark Horse Books, 2020. | Series: Plants vs. Zombies vol. 15 | Audience: Ages 8+ | Audience: Grades 4-6 | Summary: When the evil Dr. Zomboss hears of the plants' plan to destroy the zombies he comes up with a plan of his own, a plan which the plants, Crazy Dave, and Nate and Patrice, must now try and counter.
Identifiers: LCCN 2019038152 (print) | LCCN 2019038153 (ebook) | ISBN 9781506713052 (hardcover) | ISBN 9781506713144 (ebook)
Subjects: LCSH: Graphic novels. | CYAC: Graphic novels. | Zombies--Fiction. | Plants--Fiction. | Humorous stories.
Classification: LCC PZ7.7.T62 Be 2020 (print) | LCC PZ7.7.T62 (ebook) | DDC 741.5/973--dc23
LC record available at https://lccn.loc.gov/2019038152
LC ebook record available at https://lccn.loc.gov/2019038153

Written by PAUL TOBIN
Art by CHRISTIANNE GILLENARDO-GOUDREAU
Colors by HEATHER BRECKEL
Letters by STEVE DUTRO
Cover by CHRISTIANNE GILLENARDO-GOUDREAU

DARK HORSE BOOKS

PLANTS
VS.
ZOMBIES
BETTER HOMES AND GUARDENS

HERE'S THE PROBLEM.
ZOMBIE ACTION FIGURE!

YOU SEE, THERE'S LOTS OF ZOMBIES.

AND THEN THERE'S LOTS OF PLANTS.

AND BECAUSE THE ZOMBIES WANT TO EAT BRAINS, AND BECAUSE THE PLANTS WANT TO HELP PEOPLE...
...THAT MEANS THE PLANTS HAVE TO STOP THE ZOMBIES FROM GETTING TO ANY HOUSES.

"BECAUSE IF THE ZOMBIES GET TO THE HOUSES, IT'S ALL OVER."
AAAAGHHH!

BUT WHAT IF...
...WE WERE TO HAVE PLANTS *INSIDE* THE HOUSES, GUARDING *THERE*, TOO?

"I'VE PREPARED A LITTLE VISUAL AID TO LET YOU KNOW WHAT THAT WOULD BE LIKE.
HOP
HOP
HOP

"HERE WE SEE A ZOMBIE THAT, DESPITE THE PLANTS' BEST EFFORTS, REACHES THE FRONT DOOR.

"AND HE GOES INTO THE HOUSE, AND..."
BRAAAAINSS
PUSH

CUTAWAY VIEW!
P-THOOOM!
SPLATCH
AND THAT'S OUR IDEA! PLANTS GUARDING INSIDE THE HOUSES, TOO!
WE CALL THEM, "INDOOR GUARD-ENS!"
WHAT DO YOU THINK OF OUR IDEA, CRAZY DAVE?
GOOSEWHIPPLE FLOOB SPAKKLE!
SIGH UNCLE DAVE SAYS THAT...
"...HE'S BEEN MOSTLY PAYING ATTENTION TO BELCHER VON BOOMTHROAT STARRING IN THE NINTH EPISODE OF THE 'FABULOUS FROG' DATING REALITY SHOW.
"THE GIRLS LOVE HIM."
BUUUURRRP!
UNCLE DAVE ALSO THINKS OUR IDEA IS GOOD, THOUGH!

SO, NOW WE HAVE TO DECIDE ON WHAT PLANTS ARE BEST FOR THE GUARD-ENS.
HMM.
MAYBE WE SHOULD LET THE PLANTS DECIDE?
OH! GOOD IDEA!
HOW ABOUT IT, GUYS? WHO WANTS TO VOLUNTEER?
SHUFFLE
SHUFFLE
SHUFFLE
THE TEAMS ARE FORMED!
NOW IT'S TIME FOR... TRAINING! WE'LL TEACH YOU HOW TO PROPERLY GUARD A HOUSE!
ROOFTOP SENTRY!
ENTRY SENTRY!
SWEET HOME

SQUALL
SQUALL
BARK
BARK
QUACK
The mailman is actually okay!

Maybe help grandpa build his website?

DO NOT TAKE MADAME TORPEDO'S PILLOW!

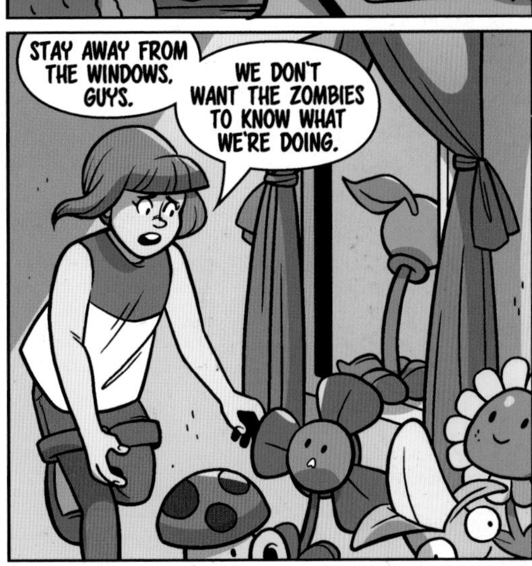
STAY AWAY FROM THE WINDOWS, GUYS.
WE DON'T WANT THE ZOMBIES TO KNOW WHAT WE'RE DOING.

HMM.

SEEMS OKAY.

SQUICK!
GASP! MR. STUBBINS! THE ZOMBIE HEDGEHOG!
Z-TECH SUCTION CUPS!
SCHEME SCHEME
Z-TECH COFFEE CUP!
SIP
SIP
ADORABLE ZOMBIE HEDGEHOG HICCUPS!
HIC
HIC
HICCUP
LEAP!
HICCUP
HICCUP
HIC HIC
PUTT
PUTT
PUTT
ROAR!
ZOOM

EANWHILE, THE ZOMBIES ARE DOING SOME TRAINING OF THEIR OWN!
NiGEL
OKAY. TODAY, WE LEARN HOW TO NOT TAKE ANY OF MY DELICIOUS BRAIN-FLAVORED POP SMARTS.
TUGBOAT, YOU GO FIRST. TRY TO TAKE ONE OF MY POP SMARTS.

LIFT!
LIFT!
REACH

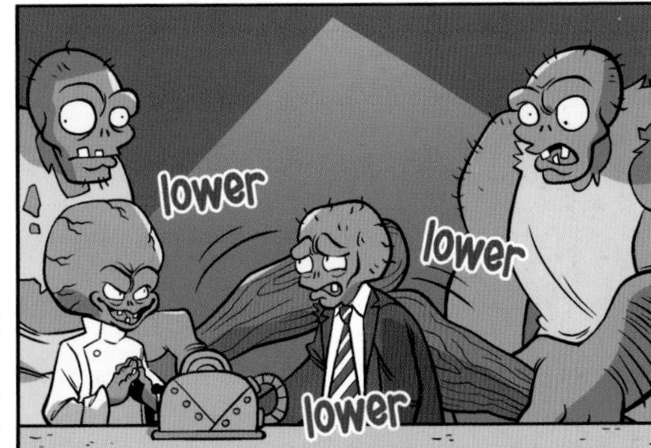
lower
lower
lower

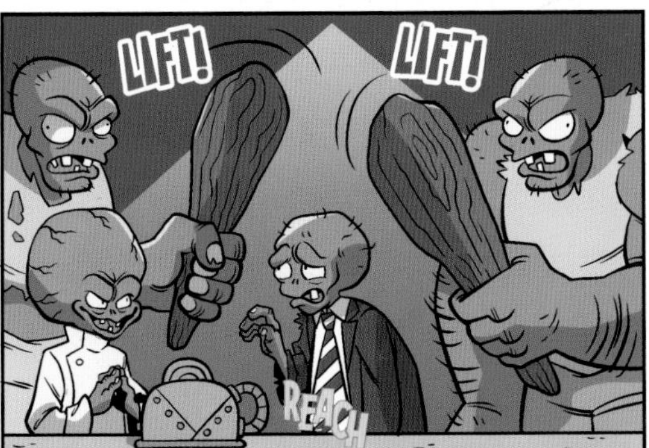
LIFT!
LIFT!
REACH

lower
lower
lower

TUGBOOOAT?

TREMBLE
TREMBLE

PUTT
ZOOM
PUTT
DESTINATION!
OBSTACLES!
BEEEP
BEEEP
OBSTACLES!
narrow
SMACK
Z-TECH CLASS 100
TOE POUNDER!
FLOINNT!
PUTT
PUTT
ZOOM
ZOOM
POUND
ZWOOOSH!

SQUICK!
HMM?
YOU SAY THAT THOSE INFERNAL KIDS AND CRAZY DAVE HAVE STARTED PUTTING PLANTS INSIDE HOUSES?
MAKING GUARD-ENS?
THIS IS A CATASTROPHE!
AND I'M THE ONLY ONE WHO GETS TO CAUSE CATASTROPHES!
SO WE'LL JUST SEE ABOUT THIS!
REACH
LIFT!
LIFT!
STAREDOWN!!!
MUNCH
MUNCH
MUNCH

AND SO, SOON...

SO, THEY'RE PUTTING PLANTS INSIDE THE HOUSES? THEN THAT IS WHERE WE WILL FIGHT!
ZOMBIE HOUSE ASSAULT TRAINING BEGINS... NOW!

FIRST, WE TRAIN ON... HOW TO SCALE A WALL!

CHEW
CHEW
CHOMP

THAT'S IT. YES. THAT'S...

FWUMPP!
THAT'S NOT IT.

NiGeL
TREMBLE
"HOW TO OPEN A WINDOW" TRAINING!
URRRR!
HRRRRN!
GUHH!
TREMBLE

NiGeL
FWOOP!
SQUICK!

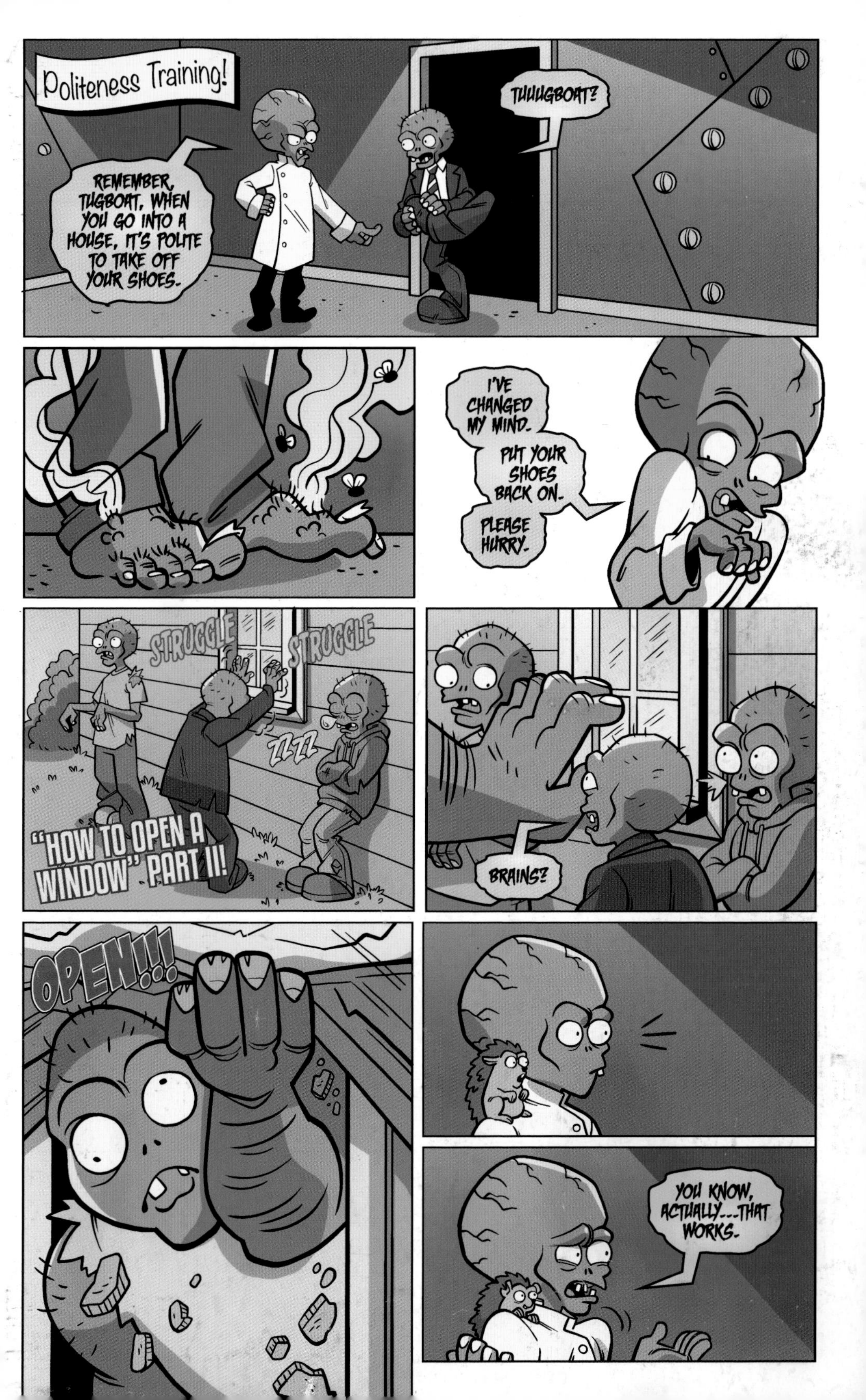
Politeness Training!
REMEMBER, TUGBOAT, WHEN YOU GO INTO A HOUSE, IT'S POLITE TO TAKE OFF YOUR SHOES.
TUUUGBOAT?
I'VE CHANGED MY MIND.
PUT YOUR SHOES BACK ON.
PLEASE HURRY.
STRUGGLE
STRUGGLE
ZZZZ
"HOW TO OPEN A WINDOW" PART II!
BRAINS?
OPEN!!!
YOU KNOW, ACTUALLY...THAT WORKS.

OKAY, ZOMBIES, WE'RE GOING TO HAVE TO ADMIT THAT, OVERALL...WE'RE NOT VERY GOOD AT THIS.
IN FACT, WE'RE NOT VERY GOOD AT A LOT OF THINGS.
"LIKE SCUBA-YODELING.
FIZZLE
"ARMPIT FARTS.
THONK!
"PIN THE TAIL ON THE DONKEY.
BRAINS?
SLUUURP
"ART CRITICISM.
"GYMNASTICS."
FLAPPP!
"COOKING."
YAAAAAWN
OR PAYING ATTENTION WHEN I'M READING A LIST.

BUT THERE ARE THINGS WE'RE GOOD AT, AND ONE OF THEM IS...
...ATTACKING THINGS!

"LIKE...WIND CHIMES!"
TING
RING
RING
TING!

"OUR OWN REFLECTIONS!

"THIS SCARECROW MADE OF FIREWORKS!
NiGG
"WELL, ACTUALLY, THIS ONE'S NOT GOING SO WELL.

"ANYWAY, MOSTLY WE'RE GOOD AT ATTACKING... PLANTS!

"BUT LET'S NOT LOSE SIGHT OF WHY WE'RE AT WAR AGAINST THE PLANTS. IT'S SO THAT WE CAN FIGHT OUR WAY TO YUMMY NUMMY BRAINS."
PEOPLE ARE IN HOUSES!
BRAINS ARE IN PEOPLE!

SO BEFORE THE PLANTS FORTIFY THE INSIDES OF THE HOUSES, LET'S FORTIFY THE INSIDES OF OUR STOMACHS WITH BRAINS.
FIRST, WE NEED TO CHOOSE A HOUSE TO ATTACK.

"HMM. NOT THAT ONE. THAT HOUSE LOOKS LIKE A BOSS BATTLE."

AND NOT THAT ONE. THAT'S MISS BLICKENDURFER'S HOUSE.
SHE'S THE ONE WHO ADOPTED MR. PIGG, THE REMARKABLY TERRITORIAL STRAY DOG.

WE DON'T WANT TO FIGHT THAT DOG.

"THAT HOUSE LOOKS TOO COLD.

"THAT HOUSE LOOKS TOO WARM.

"THAT HOUSE HAS THREE BEARS."

AH! HERE WE GO! PERFECT!
AND I DON'T SEE A SINGLE PLANT IN THE YARD!
ATTACK!
SQUICK!

ZOMBIE FOOT!
TAP!

SIGH. WELL, OKAY, THEN.
TIME FOR A GENIUS PLAN OF...

...HIDING BEHIND MY ZOMBIES!
BRAINS?
SCOOTER THE PEA-SHOOTER!
P-TOO
DING!
BANG!
DING!
DING!
BANG!
BRAINS?
OOF!
THONK!
HIGH-FIVE!
WHAP!
SLAP!
!!
GASP!

ARRRRR!
BIG TROUBLE: LARGEST OF ALL THE GARGANTUARS!
TH-WHAMMM!
DODGE
SCRAMBLE
OOG!
GRRAWRR-BEAR THE ULTIMATE FACE-PUNCHER! (HE ENJOYS PUNCHING STOMACHS, TOO!)
BELLY-BELT!!
NIGEL BLIMPBOTTOM!
TUGBOAT!
EDGAR ALLAN POTATO MINE!
SHUFFLE
FROGPANTS!
SHUFFLE
SHUFFLE
LURK
LURK
BOOOOM!
BRAINS?
OLD PHIL, THE COWBOY ZOMBIE!

BILLY SHIMMERS! DISCO CHAMPION!
JEFF THE SUNFLOWER! ACCOMPLISHED BEEKEEPER!
BUZZ
BUZZ
SHINE!
SHINE!
PATRICE BLAZING! CRAZY DAVE'S NIECE. FIERCE!
NATE TIMELY! ALSO FIERCE! (AND A LITTLE HUNGRY.)
C'MON, EVERYONE! FIRE AT WILL!
BRAINS?
WILL. (DOOMED, APPARENTLY.)
THWOOSH!
PHOOOSH
ZOOM!
ZING!
FLOOONG

HAH! WE'VE GOT THEM ON THE RUN!
?
?
ZOOM
ZOOM
ERRRRT!
!!!
OWWWW!
THOMPP!!

WHIRRRRRR!

WELL, WE WON THIS BATTLE, BUT WE'RE EXTREMELY LUCKY!
I DON'T FEEL EXTREMELY LUCKY! I FEEL EXTREMELY TOE-POUNDED!
OWW OWW OWW!

I MEAN THAT THIS WAS A RELATIVELY SMALL AMOUNT OF ZOMBIES. IF ZOMBOSS HAD SENT HIS WHOLE ARMY, WE DEFINITELY WOULD HAVE BEEN OVERWHELMED!
AND THAT MEANS...WE NEED TO GET TO WORK ON THOSE GUARD-ENS!
IT'S TIME FOR SOME...

...INTERIOR DECORATING!
KNOCK
KNOCK
KNOCK
WELCOM

HERE'S SOME PLANTS FOR YOUR ZEN GARDEN, MR. QUINN!
OOH!
WELCOM

OH! THANKS!
AND YOURS, MRS. LAGHARI!

AND FOR YOU, MR. PERSON IN A GORILLA COSTUME.
OOG!

AND SO...THE GUARD-ENS GROW!

AND GROW!

AND GROW!

Helpful health tips for indoor plant care!

NEVER GIVE THE TELEVISION PASSWORD TO TALL-NUTS! (THEY'LL HOG THE COUCH.)

OR THE INTERNET PASSWORD TO SUNFLOWERS! (THEY'LL SPEND ALL DAY POSTING SELFIES.)

AND BE AWARE THAT PEASHOOTERS WILL CONSTANTLY ORDER TAKEOUT ICE CREAM!

CRAZY DAVE INVENTION BREAK!
MY UNCLE MADE A NON-ELECTRIC TOOTHBRUSH!
ISN'T THAT JUST...A TOOTHBRUSH?

AND A PIZZA AMPLIFIER! SO, NOW YOU CAN HEAR WHAT THEY'RE SAYING!
I NEVER KNEW THEY COULD TALK!

AND THIS PIZZA TRANSLATOR, SO YOU CAN UNDERSTAND WHAT THEY'RE SAYING!
I AM LEARNING SO MANY SECRETS!

AN ELECTRONIC DISCO-ENHANCING BADGE. IT ADDS +6 TO YOUR DISCO SKILLS!
WOW...I'D BE ALL THE WAY UP TO THREE!
DISCO QUEEN!

BUT, BEST OFF, DAVE ALSO TOOK THE TIME TO MAKE A PILE OF VARIOUS BLUEPRINTS FOR GUARD-ENS.
NICE! WE CAN USE THESE!

BUT THEN...
IT'S TIME TO FIGHT THESE SO-CALLED GUARD-ENS.
IT'S TIME FOR MY...BALLOON ZOMBIES!
I HAVE EXTRA BALLOONS LATELY, THANKS TO...
"...THE LEFTOVER BALLOONS FROM THE SURPRISE PARTY MY ZOMBIES DIDN'T THROW ME.
"AND THE ONE THEY DID THROW FOR MR. STUBBINS.

"BUT NEVER MIND THAT! THERE WILL BE PLENTY OF TIME FOR ME TO CELEBRATE LATER, AFTER MY ZOMBIES CONQUER THE HOUSES!

"BY NOW, MY ZOMBIES WILL BE ATTACKING A HOUSE!

"GAINING ENTRY BY INGENIOUS MEANS! VICTORY WILL BE OURS!"

BUT THEN...
NiGeL
SHUFFLE
SHUFFLE

BRAAINSS?
FWOOP!

MELON-PULTS! CACTI! PEASHOOTERS! CHOMPERS! CABBAGE-PULTS!

AND AN ELECTRIC HORSE!
I HONESTLY DON'T KNOW WHAT THIS DOES OR WHY IT'S HERE.

NEARBY...
BING!
?
!
CLOCK!
CLOCK!
CLOCK!
CLOCK!
CLOCK!
HMM... LOOKS LIKE THE CLOCK STRUCK TWELVE!

GRAB!
WHOA!
OH, NO! SO MANY ZOMBIES!
HEY!
HOUSE RULES
No fighting after 9:00 PM!
The pancakes are mine: NO EXCEPTIONS!
NO FIGHTING AFTER 9:00 PM!
I HAVE TO WORK IN THE MORNING!
HOUSE RULES
No fighting after 9:00 PM!
The pancakes are mine:
EXCEPTIONS!

STAREDOWN!!!
SUPER DEFEATED!

BRAINS?

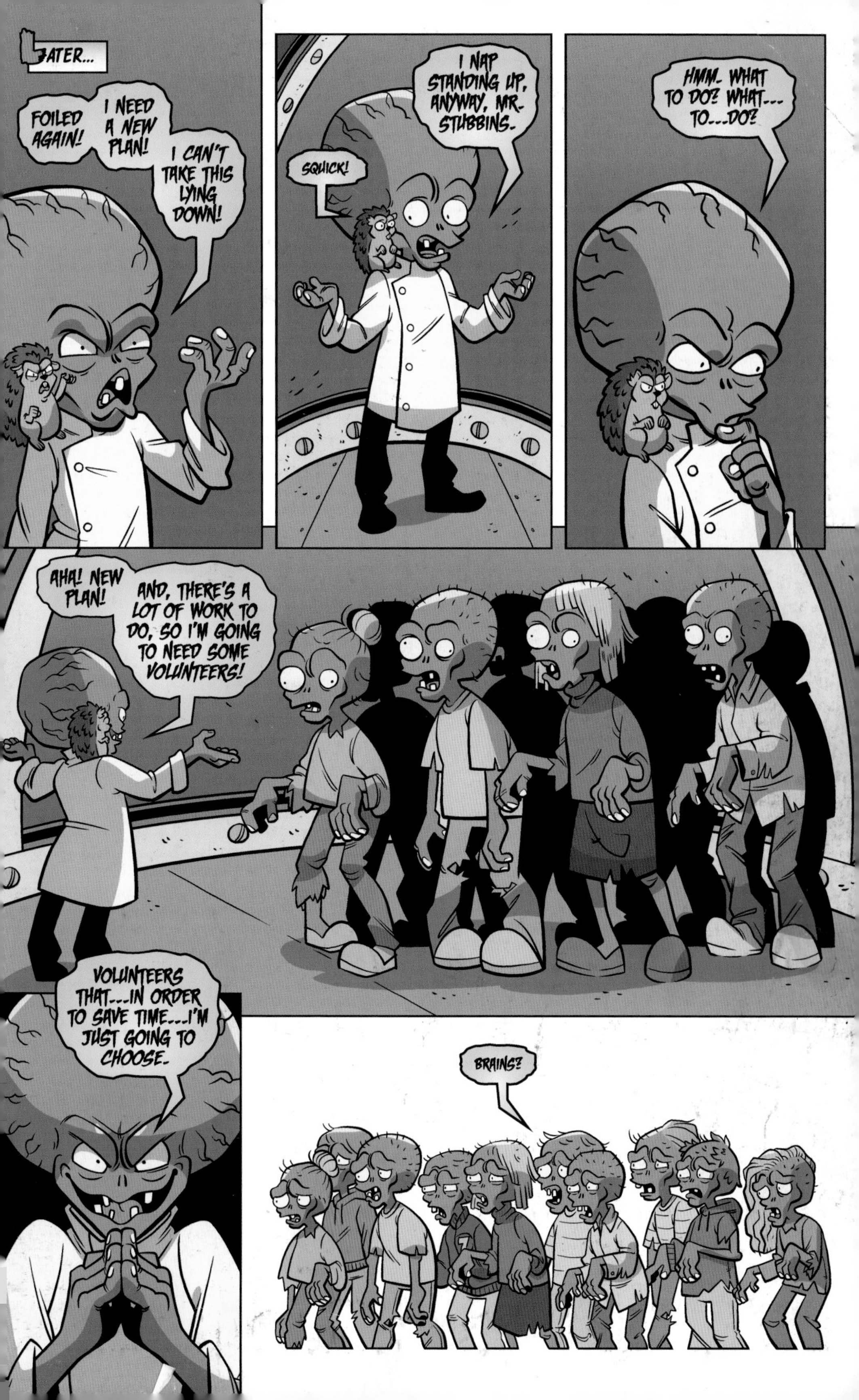
LATER...
FOILED AGAIN!
I NEED A NEW PLAN!
I CAN'T TAKE THIS LYING DOWN!
SQUICK!
I NAP STANDING UP, ANYWAY, MR. STUBBINS.
HMM. WHAT TO DO? WHAT... TO...DO?
AHA! NEW PLAN!
AND, THERE'S A LOT OF WORK TO DO, SO I'M GOING TO NEED SOME VOLUNTEERS!
VOLUNTEERS THAT...IN ORDER TO SAVE TIME...I'M JUST GOING TO CHOOSE.
BRAINS?

YOU ARE IN CHARGE OF WASHING MY SOCKS. AND DON'T HURT THE FLIES!
THEIR NAMES ARE JENNIFER, CAROLINE, AND GRENDEL, AND I LOVE THEM.
OLD PHIL, YOU ARE IN CHARGE OF APPLYING MY UNDERWORLD DEODORANT™ SO THAT I WILL SMELL LIKE DELICIOUSLY FRESH SOIL AND WORMS.
squidge
squidge
YOU ARE IN CHARGE OF PICKING ALL THE RAISINS OUT OF MY RAISIN BRAIN CEREAL.
Raisin Brain
pick
pick
pick
I REALLY ONLY LIKE THE BRAINS.
NIGEL BLIMPBOTTOM FROGPANTS, AND TUGBOAT, YOU ARE IN CHARGE OF PRETENDING TO BE REALTORS...
...THE PROFESSION OF THOSE WHO SELL HOUSES.
NiGeL
AND I.... I WILL CREATE BETTER HOMES FOR THE HUMANS!
?

BETTER FOR ME, ANYWAY!
"BECAUSE ONCE THE YUMMY CITIZENS TAKE UP RESIDENCE...
WELCOME
"...THEY'LL DISCOVER MY INGENIOUS SURPRISE!"
SLAMM!
"AND HOW THEY'VE BEEN ADDED TO A TAKEOUT MENU, WITH THE HOMES..."
RUMBLE
RUMBLE
CLANG
CLANG
CLANG
"...DELIVERING THEIR DELICIOUS BRAINS TO THE CLUTCHES OF MY ZOMBIE HORDES!"
GET IN LINE BEHIND ME! BEHIND ME!
DING DING DING! DINNER TIME!

SOON...
HERE, MR. STUBBINS! I'VE FINISHED THIS WORKING PROTOTYPE!
THESE VOLUNTEERS WILL HELP DEMONSTRATE HOW IT WORKS!

PUTT
PUTT PUTT
SPUTTER SPUTTER
CLANG

THUMP

BOOOOM!

BRAINS?
WELL, I STILL HAVE TO WORK OUT SOME OF THE DETAILS, BUT YOU GET THE PICTURE.

OKAY! LET'S GET TO WORK! AND FIRST OF ALL... YOU NEED WORK CLOTHES!
IF YOU'RE GOING TO DRESS LIKE HUMAN REALTORS, YOU'LL NEED...

...THESE SUITS!
BRAINS?

THAT'S RIGHT, TUGBOAT. I KNOW IT SEEMS AMAZING, BUT...
...THERE ARE CLOTHES THAT DON'T HAVE HOLES IN THEM.

AND NOW, LET'S GET YOU THE SECOND PART OF YOUR DISGUISES...
BUSINESS CARDS!

Nigel Blimpbottom
Not Fake Realtor
Ask Me About Brains!
(please don't ask me anything else)
Z TECH

Frogpants
Trustworthy Not Zombie Realtor
Neighborville's #1 Most Trusted Name in Selling Dangerous Houses to Unsuspecting Humans.

Tugboat?

Tugbooooaaat?

Brains?

I sell houses.

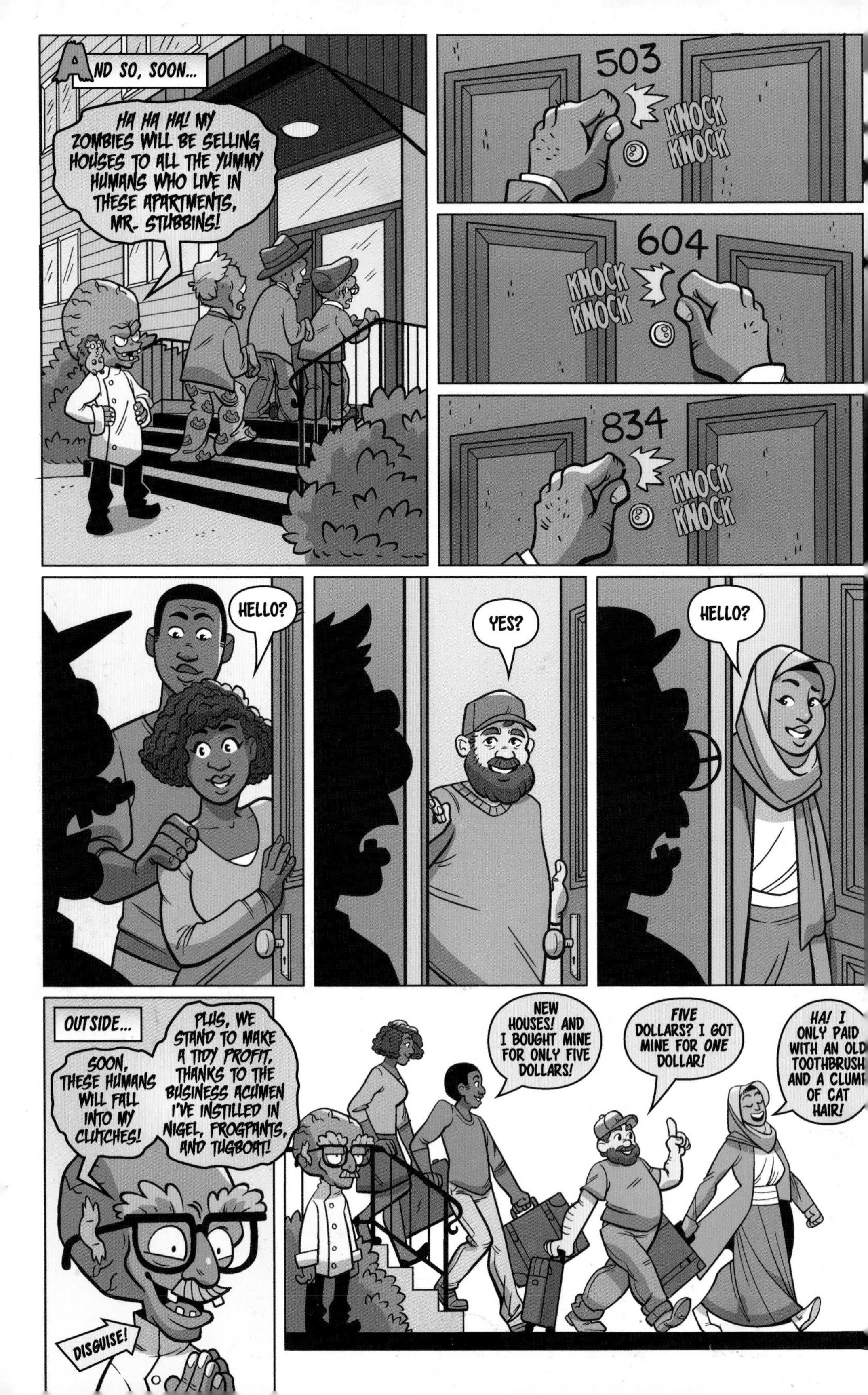
AND SO, SOON...
HA HA HA! MY ZOMBIES WILL BE SELLING HOUSES TO ALL THE YUMMY HUMANS WHO LIVE IN THESE APARTMENTS, MR. STUBBINS!
503
KNOCK KNOCK
604
KNOCK KNOCK
834
KNOCK KNOCK
HELLO?
YES?
HELLO?
OUTSIDE...
SOON, THESE HUMANS WILL FALL INTO MY CLUTCHES!
PLUS, WE STAND TO MAKE A TIDY PROFIT, THANKS TO THE BUSINESS ACUMEN I'VE INSTILLED IN NIGEL, FROGPANTS, AND TUGBOAT!
DISGUISE!
NEW HOUSES! AND I BOUGHT MINE FOR ONLY FIVE DOLLARS!
FIVE DOLLARS? I GOT MINE FOR ONE DOLLAR!
HA! I ONLY PAID WITH AN OLD TOOTHBRUSH AND A CLUMP OF CAT HAIR!

HMMM. WELL, PERHAPS WE WON'T MAKE A PROFIT, BUT WE'LL STILL CAPTURE SOME HUMANS.

HMM? UH-OH. TRY NOT TO LOOK SUSPICIOUS.

?
?
?

RUMBLE
HELLO?
!
RUMBLE
!
!
CLANG
WHAT'S GOING ON?
RUMBLE

RUMBLE
CLANG
CLANG
RUMBLE

JUST... KEEP TRYING NOT TO LOOK SUSPICIOUS.
I DON'T THINK THE PLANTS NOTICED ANYTHING!

GEAR
UNCLE DAVE! THE PLANTS SAY THEY SAW ZOMBOSS!
HE'S...SELLING WEIRD HOUSES TO PEOPLE!
BROPCOGGLE? PIMENTO DIBBLESTOOP!
WHAT'D CRAZY DAVE SAY?
HE SAYS HE'S THINKING HARD ON A SOLUTION!
SQUELPBELLY HOWITZER CHOMP!
DID HE SOLVE IT? WHAT'D HE SAY?
UH, HE SAYS HE'S JUST INVENTED...
"...FABULOUS FLYING FRENCH FRIES THAT WILL DIVE RIGHT INTO YOUR MOUTH!"
SLAPP!
PERFECT! THAT SOLVES IT!
UH, GUYS?
NO.

SOON...
WHAT WE NEED TO DO IS GET MY UNCLE DAVE TO START BUILDING BETTER HOUSES...
...SO THAT EVERYONE DOESN'T MOVE INTO THOSE HOUSE-TRAPS ZOMBOSS IS MAKING.
THE PROBLEM IS, MY UNCLE IS...,STRANGE, SO IT'S *OUR* JOB TO MAKE SURE HE'S BUILDING A GOOD HOUSE.

GIANT ICE CREAM MACHINE HOUSE
THIS ONE'S *GOOD!*
UH... I DON'T THINK SO.

DISCO HOUSE!!!
IT'S PERFECT!
I'M... DEFINITELY *NOT* GOING TO GIVE THIS A PASSING GRADE.

THE HOVERING TURTLE HOUSE!!!
ALL THESE *TURTLES! HOVERING!* IT'S *GREAT!*
NATE.
SERIOUSLY.
NO.

SOON...
AH, NOW HERE'S A GOOD HOUSE!
NICE WORK, UNCLE DAVE!
AWW, I THINK IT NEEDS A PIZZA PARLOR, WITH DOGS FOR WAITERS!

AND...
ANOTHER GOOD HOUSE, UNCLE DAVE! I LOVE THE WINDOWS!
I'M NOT SEEING ANY MISSILE LAUNCHERS. WHY AREN'T THERE ANY MISSILE LAUNCHERS?

AND IT NEEDS A SECRET ROOM SPECIFICALLY FOR PLAYING VIDEO GAMES!
PLUS THE WALLS SHOULD BE MADE OF CHOCOLATE. OR GRILLED CHEESE.
AND THE HOUSE CAN FLY. WITH ROCKETS.

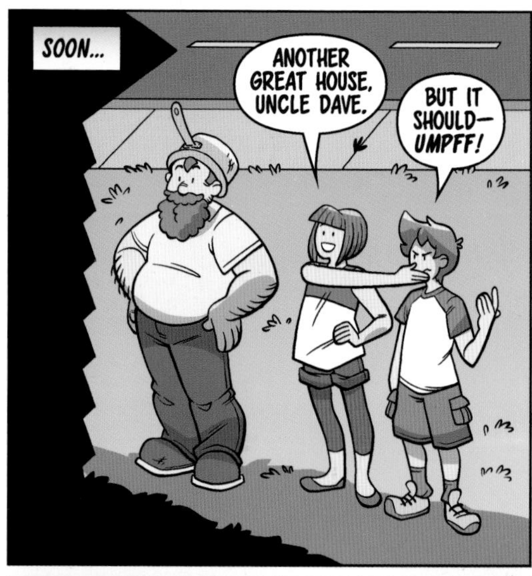
SOON...
ANOTHER GREAT HOUSE, UNCLE DAVE.
BUT IT SHOULD—UMPFF!

AND...
AND ANOTHER FANTASTIC HOUSE, UNCLE DAVE. HOUSE #12 IS FANTASTIC!
YOU'RE ON A ROLL!
GURKK!

PLUS...
PERFECT! HOUSE #15 LOOKS FANTASTIC!
I WOULDN'T CHANGE A THING!
URFF!

AND SO...
GAHHH! PEOPLE ARE LIVING IN CRAZY DAVE'S NICE CHARMING HOUSES, NOW, INSTEAD OF MOVING INTO MY DEVIOUS HOUSE-TRAPS!
HOW CAN I ENTICE THEM AWAY? WHAT CAN I DO?
NiGeL

HMM. WHEN I NEED ADVICE, THERE'S ONE SOURCE THAT I TRUST MORE THAN ANYWHERE ELSE.

NIGEL!
NiGe
HAND ME MY MAGIC Z-BALL, WOULD YOU?

BECAUSE THIS ALWAYS GIVES ME THE BEST ADVICE.
SHAKE
SHAKE

HMM. YES. ALWAYS GOOD ADVICE.
Conquer

AGAIN? YES. WISE.
Conquer

A THIRD TIME? I COULDN'T AGREE MORE.
Conquer

HMM?
Soon

SOON?
WHAT DOES "SOON" MEAN?

Soon.

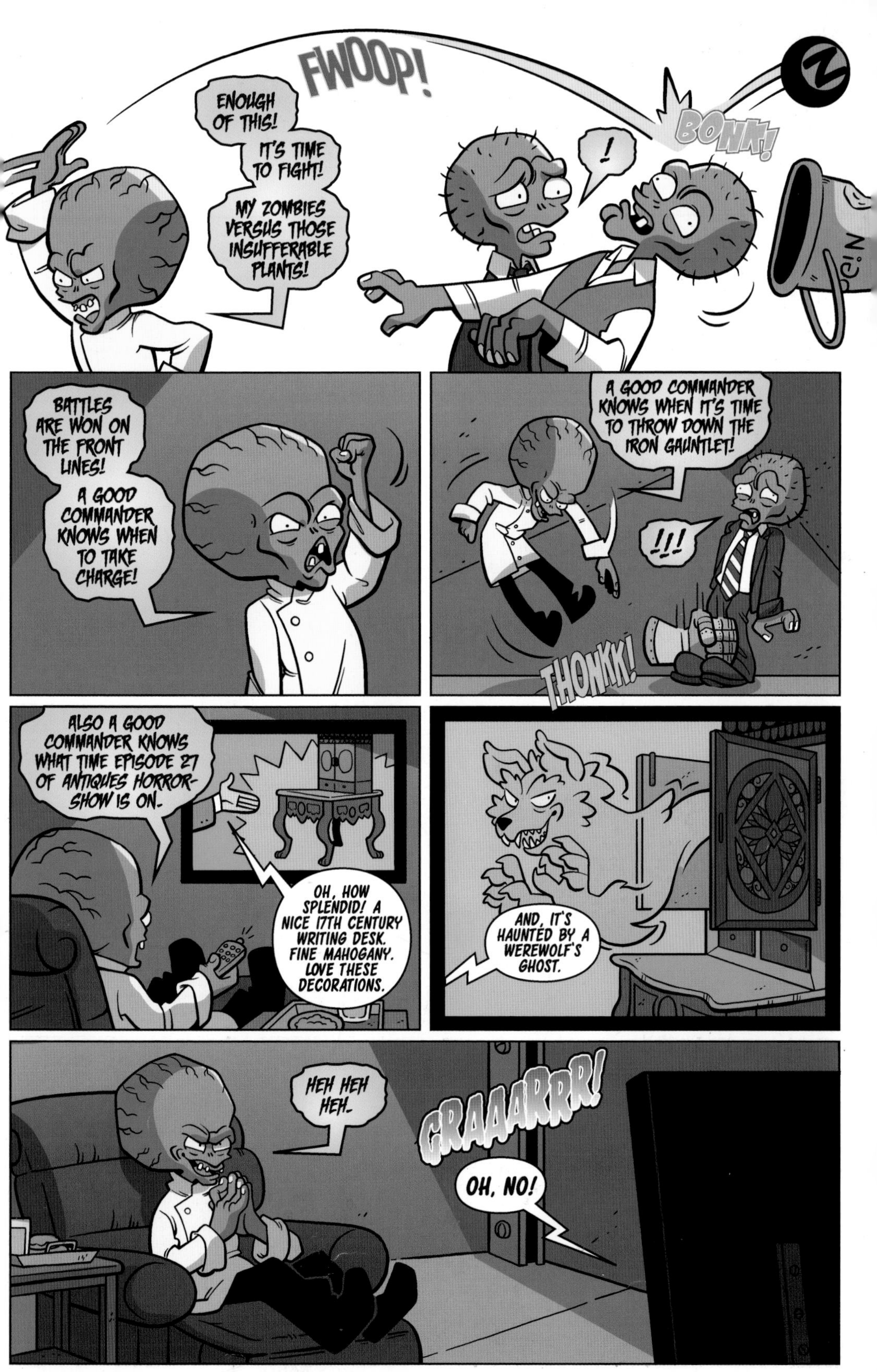
FWOOP!
ENOUGH OF THIS!
IT'S TIME TO FIGHT!
MY ZOMBIES VERSUS THOSE INSUFFERABLE PLANTS!
!
BONK!
BATTLES ARE WON ON THE FRONT LINES!
A GOOD COMMANDER KNOWS WHEN TO TAKE CHARGE!
A GOOD COMMANDER KNOWS WHEN IT'S TIME TO THROW DOWN THE IRON GAUNTLET!
!!!
THONKK!
ALSO A GOOD COMMANDER KNOWS WHAT TIME EPISODE 27 OF ANTIQUES HORROR-SHOW IS ON.
OH, HOW SPLENDID! A NICE 17TH CENTURY WRITING DESK. FINE MAHOGANY. LOVE THESE DECORATIONS.
AND, IT'S HAUNTED BY A WEREWOLF'S GHOST.
HEH HEH HEH.
GRAAARRR!
OH, NO!

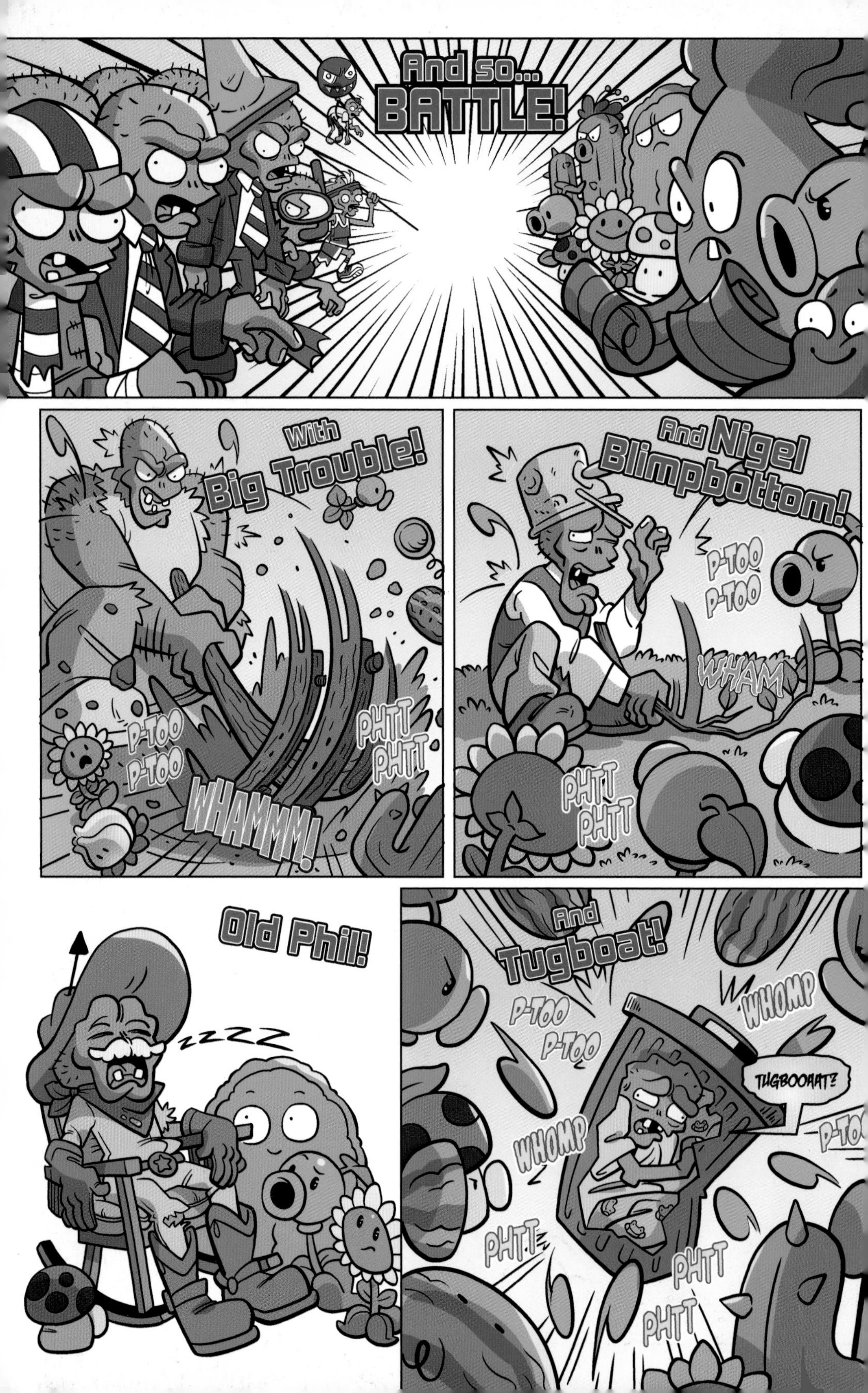
And so...
BATTLE!
With
Big Trouble!
P-TOO
P-TOO
WHAMMM!
PHTT
PHTT
And Nigel
Blimpbottom!
P-TOO
P-TOO
WHAM
PHTT
PHTT
Old Phil!
ZZZZZ
And
Tugboat!
P-TOO
P-TOO
WHOMP
TUGBOOAAT?
WHOMP
PHTT
PHTT
PHTT

And
Mr. Stubbins!
SQUICK!
VROOM
VROOM
SWERVE!
OWW!
AGAIN?
POUND
WHOMP
P-TOO
P-TOO
PHTT
PHTT
PHTT
THWOOSH
FWOOOM
ZING
ZING
ZIP!
FWOOOM
SMACK
THOOOM
FWOOSH
!
?
KRAKKA-
BOOOM!
!

ERRRRT!
SKIDDDDDDDD
GAHH!
SERIOUSLY?
POUND
THWOOOP!
WHOOOSH
THWONK
SPIN!
!!
THWOOOM!
SOMEBODY STOP THAT ZOMBIE HEDGEHOG!
SQUICK!
SOAR

SMACK

SKLORTCH!
!
!
?

SQUICK!

WHUMP!

WHUMP!
WHUMP!
WHUMP!
WHUMP!

GOOD WORK, NATE!
YOU MANAGED TO HIT HIM WITH THE FABULOUS FLYING FRENCH FRIES!
YEAH. I SUPPOSE THAT'S A GOOD THING.

BUT I WAS AIMING THEM FOR MY *MOUTH.*

LATER...
DON'T BE SAD, MR. STUBBINS. THIS FIGHT ISN'T OVER.
THIS FIGHT WILL NEVER BE OVER, BECAUSE MY MAGNIFICENT BRAIN WILL NEVER REST UNTIL MY MAGNIFICENT TUMMY GETS SOME BRAINS.
I BELIEVE... I BELIEVE IT'S TIME TO MODIFY MY PLAN WITH THE HOUSES.
"MY MISTAKE WAS IN MAKING THE HOUSES JUST LOOK PRETTY."
BUT IT'S NOT ENOUGH TO JUST LOOK PRETTY, AND I SHOULD KNOW.
NO, I MUST MAKE THE HOUSES DO MORE.
I MUST MAKE THE HOUSES FIGHT THE PLANTS WITH US!
AND SO, I WILL MAKE...

"A HOUSE WITH A GIANT UMBRELLA TO BLOCK SUNSHINE FROM PLANTS!

"A DESERT HOUSE WITH NO WATER, SO THE PLANTS WILL WITHER!

"A HOUSE WITH A GARAGE WHERE MY BAND CAN PRACTICE, SINCE WE GOT KICKED OUT OF THE COMMUNITY CENTER!"
BANG
CRASH
THUBBA
WOMP!

"A HOUSE MADE ENTIRELY OF ZOMBIES!"

TREMBLE
TREMBLE
TREMBLE

OKAY, MAYBE NOT THAT LAST ONE.

ELSEWHERE...
NATE, HAVE YOU SEEN THOSE HOUSES ZOMBOSS IS BUILDING?
WE CAN'T LET HIM GET AWAY WITH THIS!
YOU'RE RIGHT! THERE'S NO WAY I WANT TO LIVE NEXT TO THE HOUSE WHERE HIS BAND IS PRACTICING.

WE HAVE TO DESIGN SOME HOUSES THAT MY UNCLE DAVE CAN BUILD.
LET'S GET TO WORK!

SCRIBBLE
DRAW
SCRIBBLE
DRAW

THERE. I'VE DESIGNED A SERIES OF HOUSES THAT I THINK WOULD HELP, AND DRAFTED THEIR BLUEPRINTS FOR CONSTRUCTION.
WHAT HAVE YOU DONE?

I DREW THIS CARTOON OF ME EATING PIZZA.

THAT'S ME.

AND SO, SOON...
HOUSE WITH ZOMBIE ALERT SIREN!

HOUSE WITH TREADMILL DRIVEWAY!
BRAINS?
SHUFFLE
SHUFFLE
SHUFFLE
SHUFFLE
SHUFFLE
URRRRR
URRRRR

HOUSE WITH NATE EATING PIZZA!
WAVE WAVE
CHOMP! CHOMP!

HOUSE WITH PET-MOUNTED MOBILE INDOOR GUARD-ENS!
WOOF!
WHUFF!

UNFORTUNATELY...
OH! SO CRAZY DAVE THINKS HIS HOUSES CAN BEAT MINE?
WELL, WHAT IF I ADD IN SOME OF THIS, AND A LITTLE OF THAT, AND...?

MEANWHILE...
WOW, LOOK AT UNCLE DAVE GO!
SCRIBBLE
SCRIBBLE
SCRIBBLE

HAH! IF I ADD MORE HERE, AND AN ENGINE HERE, AND THEN...
HMM...WAIT. AM I GOING OVERBOARD?

NO! I'M NOT GOING OVERBOARD ENOUGH!
I WILL GO EXTRA OVERBOARD!

ARE THESE BLUEPRINTS WHAT I THINK THEY ARE?
IF YOU'RE THINKING THESE ARE PLANS FOR A GIANT WAFFLE IRON, THEN...YES.
BUT... OH, MY GOSH... UNCLE DAVE? THESE BLUEPRINTS?

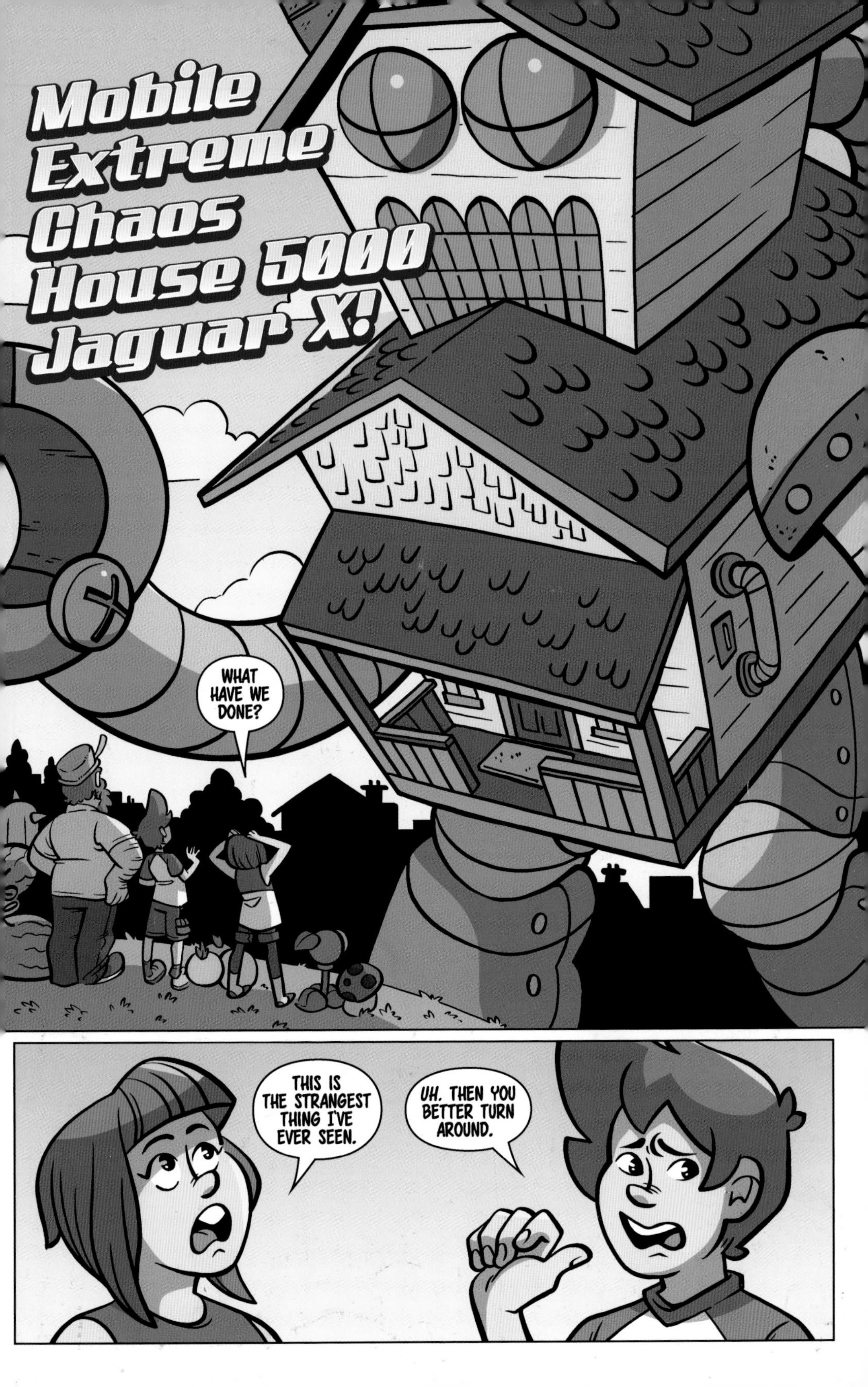
Mobile Extreme Chaos House 5000 Jaguar X!
WHAT HAVE WE DONE?
THIS IS THE STRANGEST THING I'VE EVER SEEN.
UH. THEN YOU BETTER TURN AROUND.

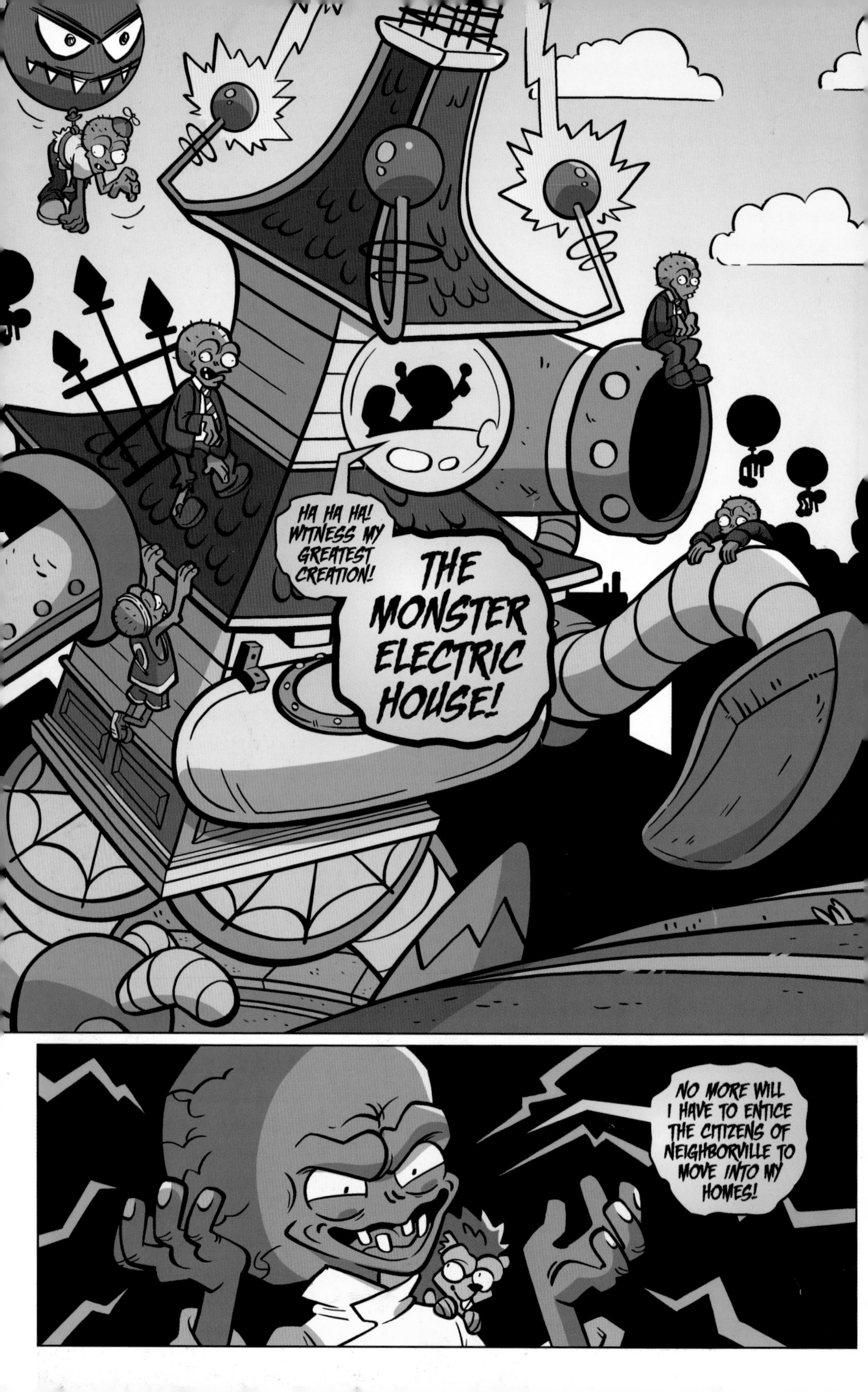
HA HA HA! WITNESS MY GREATEST CREATION!
THE MONSTER ELECTRIC HOUSE!
NO MORE WILL I HAVE TO ENTICE THE CITIZENS OF NEIGHBORVILLE TO MOVE INTO MY HOMES!

"BECAUSE NOW..."
SCOOP!

...THE HOUSE ITSELF WILL MOVE THEM INTO IT!

POUR!!!
DANG!

HA HA HA! MY NEW INVENTION HAS EVERYTHING! LIKE...A PRISON TO HOLD PEOPLE UNTIL I CAN CHOMP THEIR BRAINS!
AND THIS TWENTY-TON MISSILE-FIST!
FWOOSH
NO!
"THIS FABULOUS ZOMBIE-FIRING CANNON!"
HEE HEE GIGGLE
FF-THOOOOMM!!
NO!
"AND THESE SPEAKERS TO BLARE MY LATEST ALBUM!"
Woo woo woo Would you say it's insane?
The way way way that I love your brain
NOOOOOOO!!!

POP!
I ALSO HAVE THIS 132-SLOT POP SMART TOASTER, FOR WHEN I'M FEELING PECKISH.
POP!
POP!
POP!

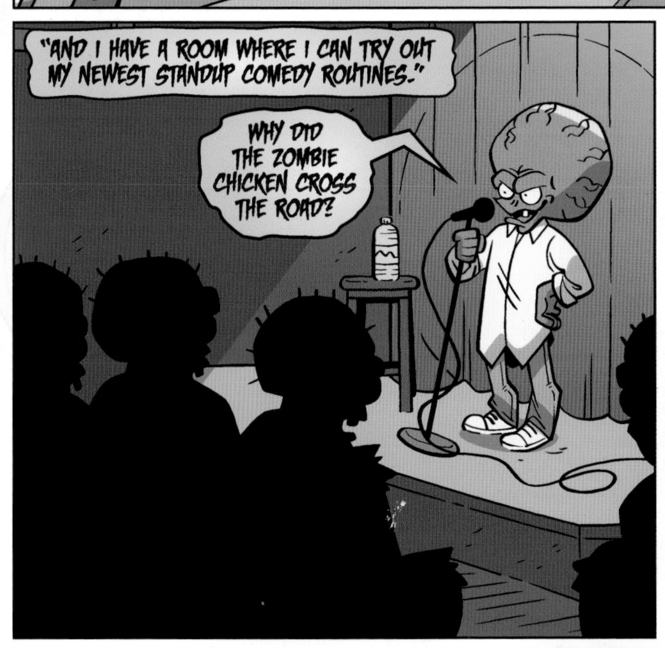
"AND I HAVE A ROOM WHERE I CAN TRY OUT MY NEWEST STANDUP COMEDY ROUTINES."
WHY DID THE ZOMBIE CHICKEN CROSS THE ROAD?

TO CONQUER EVERYONE AND EAT THEIR BRAINS.

AND MY NEW GIANT ROBOT HOUSE ALSO COMES COMPLETE WITH THIS HAIR DRYER, TO KEEP ALL THREE OF MY HAIRS IN PRISTINE CONDITION!

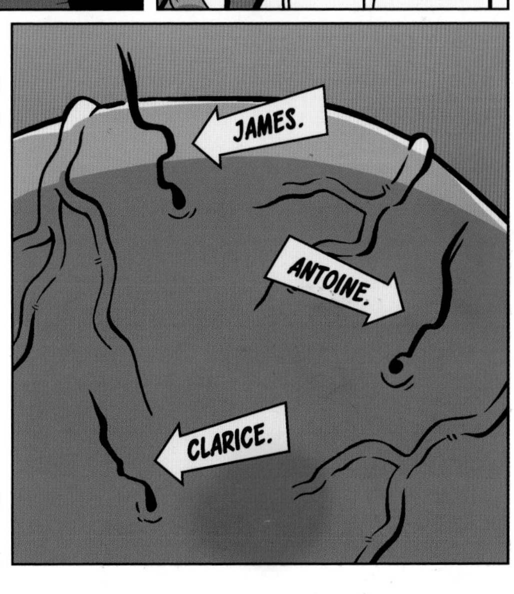
JAMES.
ANTOINE.
CLARICE.

HA! YOUR GIANT ROBOT HOUSE IS NOTHING!
WE'VE GOT...

...THIS ROOM FOR THE ELECTRIC HORSE!
STILL NOT SURE WHAT THIS THING IS FOR.

AND A MOWLING ALLEY!
MOW
MOW
MOW

AND A TWICE CREAM DISPENSER!
TWICE CREAM IS TWICE AS GOOD AS ICE CREAM!
TWICE CREAM

HEY.
WHAT ARE YOU EATING?
SOME THRICE CREAM.

OOOH!
SLURP
CHOMP
YUM
THRICE CREAM
THREE TIMES BETTER THAN ICE CREAM!

WE'VE ALSO GOT A DISCO ROOM.
THIS IS A GREAT IDEA!
SPARKLE
KA-BANGG!
FWOOSH
B-BOOM!
SIZZLE
THIS IS MAYBE NOT A GREAT IDEA!
KER-CRACK!
NATE ALSO WANTED THIS FIREWORKS ROOM.
SNOZZLE
SPAKK SPAKK
BUT MOSTLY OUR GIANT ROBOT HAS MISSILE LAUNCHERS, AND PLANT ATTACK MODULES, AND OF COURSE...
"...THE SEVENTY TON DISCO BALL OF MAMMOTH DESTRUCTION."
WHIRRR
WHIRRR
WAIT!

UNCLE DAVE! THIS IS PATRICE! YOU CAN'T ATTACK YET!
NOT WITH ALL THOSE POOR PEOPLE TRAPPED INSIDE THE M.E.H.!
C'MON, NATE! WE NEED TO ASSEMBLE A SQUAD OF EXTREMELY TALENTED PLANTS TO RESCUE THE PRISONERS!
"OKAY! I CHOOSE...
"...GRRAWRR-BEAR THE ULTIMATE FACE PUNCHER! AND FRED THE SUNFLOWER!
"AND WALLY THE TALL-NUT! AND EDGAR ALLAN POTATO MINE!
"AND SCOOTER! AND THE MELON COLLIE!"

LET'S RESCUE EVERYONE!

WAIT!
BEFORE WE GO...

...WE NEED TO CHOOSE A TEAM TO EAT ALL THIS PIZZA!

I CHOOSE... NATE!

AND NATE TIMELY!

AND... ALSO NATE.

AND...HMM... YOU KNOW WHAT?
NATE!

WOW! THANKS FOR HAVING FAITH IN ME!
I CAN DO THIS!

GOBBLE GOBBLE
GOBBLE GOBBLE

MEANWHILE...
OOH.
GOSH.
WOW.
≡GULP≡
I DON'T THINK I WANT TO MOVE INTO EITHER OF THESE NEW HOUSES.
NOPE! ME NEITHER!
I ACTUALLY LIKE MY APARTMENT!
MY CAT WOULD BE MAD IF WE MOVED.
I JUST GOT MY GAME CONSOLES ALL SET UP!
MEOW WOW
LET'S JUST LEAVE.
I TOTALLY AGREE!
MEOW WOW
TIME TO FEED MY CAT.

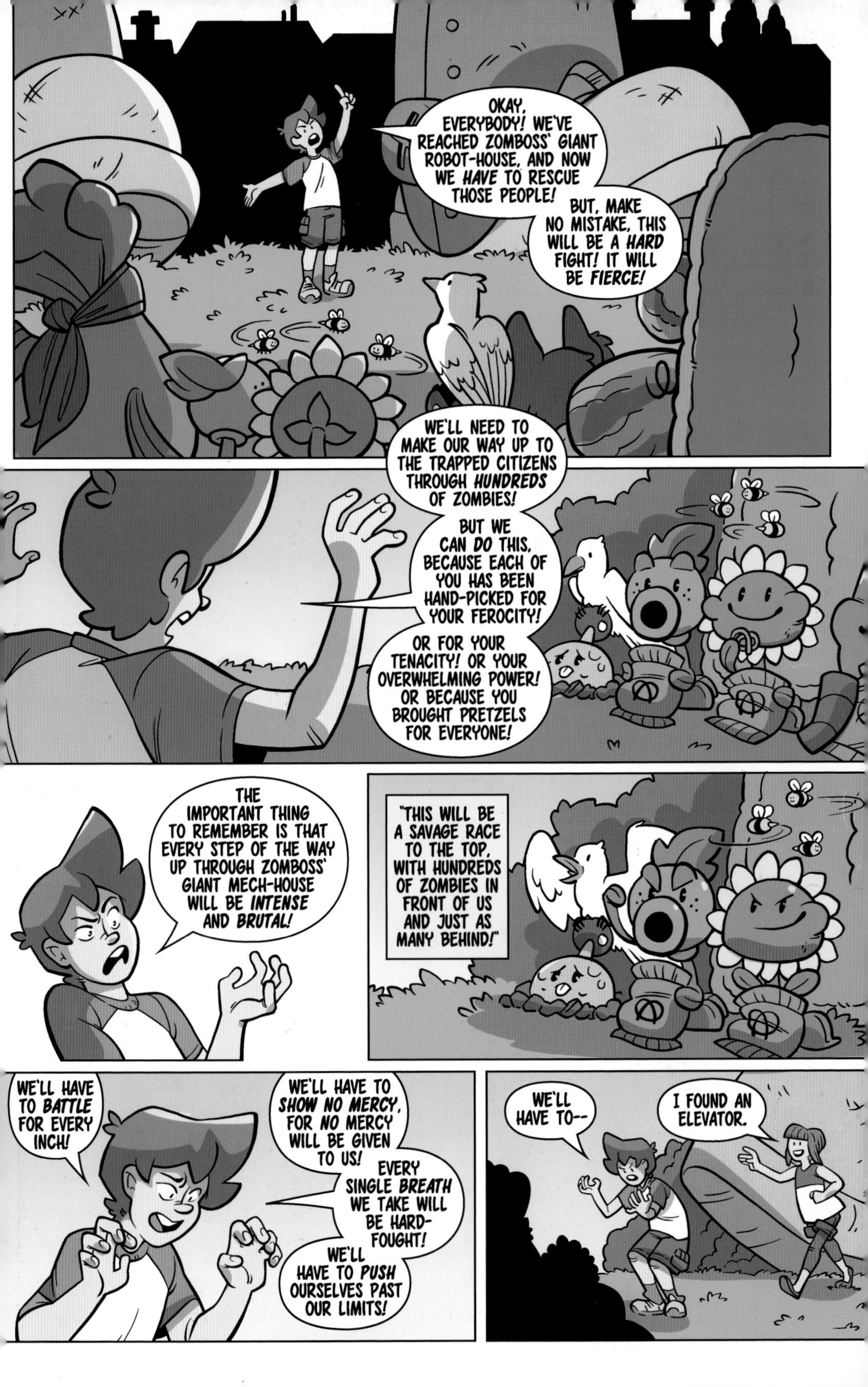
OKAY, EVERYBODY! WE'VE REACHED ZOMBOSS' GIANT ROBOT-HOUSE, AND NOW WE HAVE TO RESCUE THOSE PEOPLE!
BUT, MAKE NO MISTAKE, THIS WILL BE A HARD FIGHT! IT WILL BE FIERCE!
WE'LL NEED TO MAKE OUR WAY UP TO THE TRAPPED CITIZENS THROUGH HUNDREDS OF ZOMBIES!
BUT WE CAN DO THIS, BECAUSE EACH OF YOU HAS BEEN HAND-PICKED FOR YOUR FEROCITY!
OR FOR YOUR TENACITY! OR YOUR OVERWHELMING POWER! OR BECAUSE YOU BROUGHT PRETZELS FOR EVERYONE!
THE IMPORTANT THING TO REMEMBER IS THAT EVERY STEP OF THE WAY UP THROUGH ZOMBOSS' GIANT MECH-HOUSE WILL BE INTENSE AND BRUTAL!
"THIS WILL BE A SAVAGE RACE TO THE TOP, WITH HUNDREDS OF ZOMBIES IN FRONT OF US AND JUST AS MANY BEHIND!"
WE'LL HAVE TO BATTLE FOR EVERY INCH!
WE'LL HAVE TO SHOW NO MERCY, FOR NO MERCY WILL BE GIVEN TO US!
EVERY SINGLE BREATH WE TAKE WILL BE HARD-FOUGHT!
WE'LL HAVE TO PUSH OURSELVES PAST OUR LIMITS!
WE'LL HAVE TO--
I FOUND AN ELEVATOR.

HUH?
YEAH. HERE IT IS.
GOES STRAIGHT TO THE FLOOR WITH THE TRAPPED PEOPLE.
UH... OKAY.
OH.
MUNCH
MUNCH
MUNCH
MUNCH
MUNCH
MUNCH
MUNCH
MUNCH
IF THERE'S ANYBODY WHO DOESN'T WANT THEIR PRETZELS, I'LL TAKE THEM.

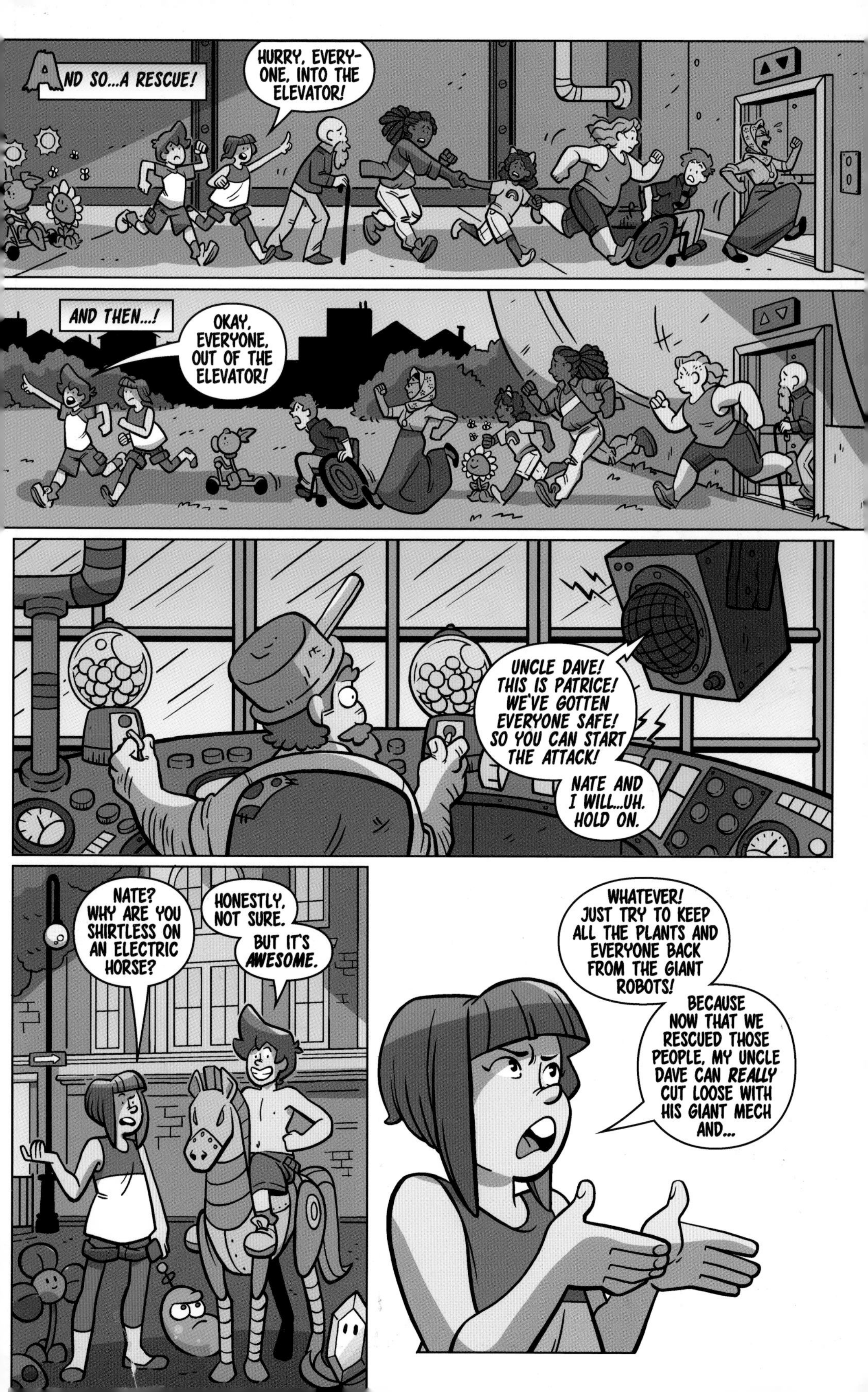
AND SO...A RESCUE!
HURRY, EVERYONE, INTO THE ELEVATOR!
AND THEN...!
OKAY, EVERYONE, OUT OF THE ELEVATOR!
UNCLE DAVE! THIS IS PATRICE! WE'VE GOTTEN EVERYONE SAFE! SO YOU CAN START THE ATTACK!
NATE AND I WILL...UH. HOLD ON.
NATE? WHY ARE YOU SHIRTLESS ON AN ELECTRIC HORSE?
HONESTLY, NOT SURE.
BUT IT'S AWESOME.
WHATEVER! JUST TRY TO KEEP ALL THE PLANTS AND EVERYONE BACK FROM THE GIANT ROBOTS!
BECAUSE NOW THAT WE RESCUED THOSE PEOPLE, MY UNCLE DAVE CAN REALLY CUT LOOSE WITH HIS GIANT MECH AND...

dance!

HUH?
WHAT?
DANCE?

UNCLE DAVE. I WAS ACTUALLY THINKING YOU'D FIGHT.

...

THUMBS UP!

FIGHT
PAP!

disco ball and chain!
SKRUNCHH!
ZOMBIE CANNON!
PHOOM!
PHOOM!
PHOOOOM!
TERRIBLE MUSIC!
FWOOSH
WHOOSH
MISSLES!

BUH-THOOOOOM!!
KEEP CLEAR EVERYONE!
ZOMBOSS ISN'T BEING TOO CAREFUL ABOUT WHERE HE STEPS!
FWOOOSH!
OH, NO! MY ICE CREAM!
SPLAT
WHEW! STILL GOOD!
RUST
RUST
OH, NO! SOMEBODY ELSE'S ICE CREAM!
WHEW! IT'S OKAY!
FTTP!
RUST
RUST
RUST
RUST
OH, NO! SOMEBODY'S PIZZA!
!!

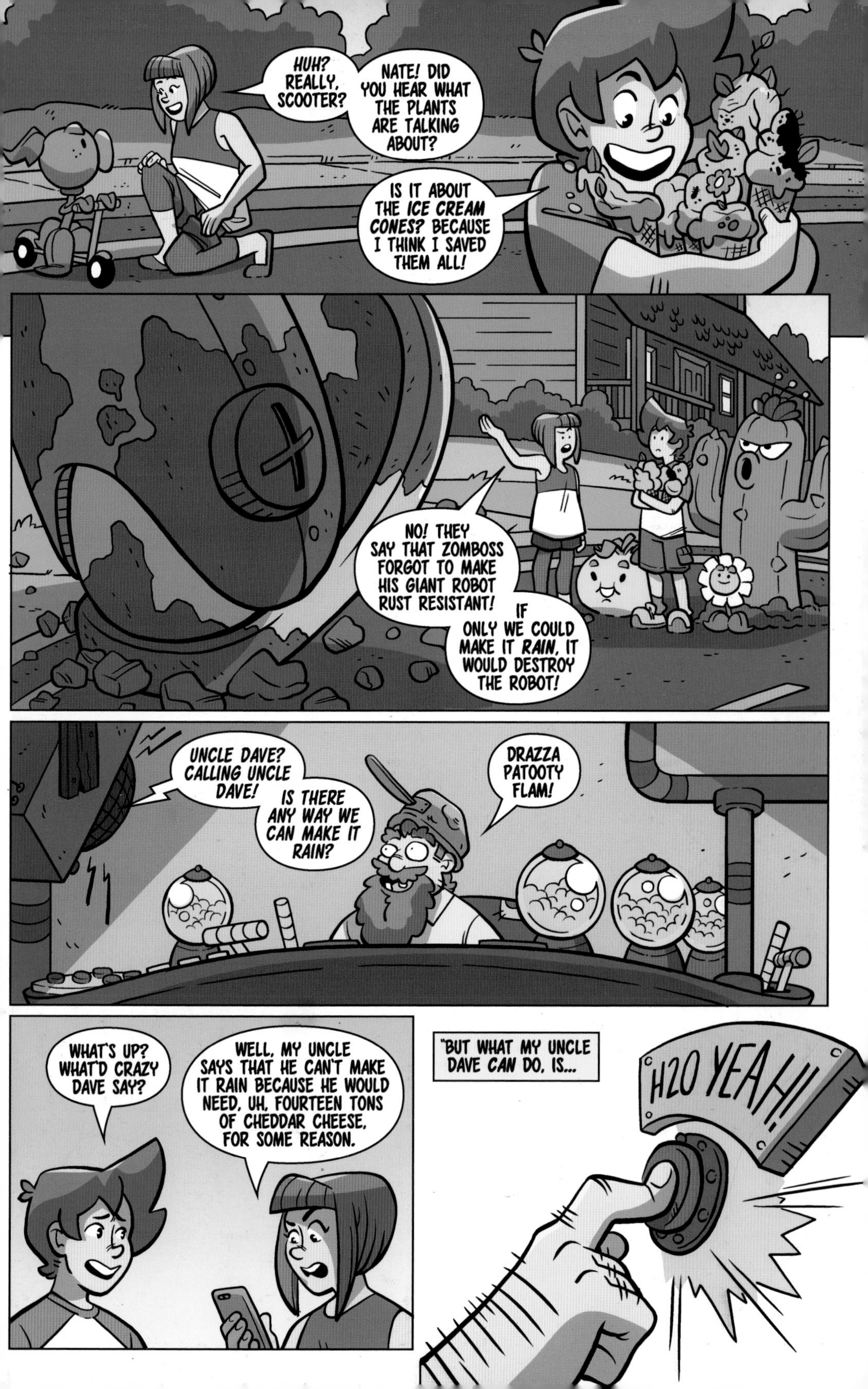
HUH? REALLY, SCOOTER?
NATE! DID YOU HEAR WHAT THE PLANTS ARE TALKING ABOUT?
IS IT ABOUT THE ICE CREAM CONES? BECAUSE I THINK I SAVED THEM ALL!
NO! THEY SAY THAT ZOMBOSS FORGOT TO MAKE HIS GIANT ROBOT RUST RESISTANT!
IF ONLY WE COULD MAKE IT RAIN, IT WOULD DESTROY THE ROBOT!
UNCLE DAVE? CALLING UNCLE DAVE!
IS THERE ANY WAY WE CAN MAKE IT RAIN?
DRAZZA PATOOTY FLAM!
WHAT'S UP? WHAT'D CRAZY DAVE SAY?
WELL, MY UNCLE SAYS THAT HE CAN'T MAKE IT RAIN BECAUSE HE WOULD NEED, UH, FOURTEEN TONS OF CHEDDAR CHEESE, FOR SOME REASON.
"BUT WHAT MY UNCLE DAVE CAN DO, IS...
H2O YEAH!

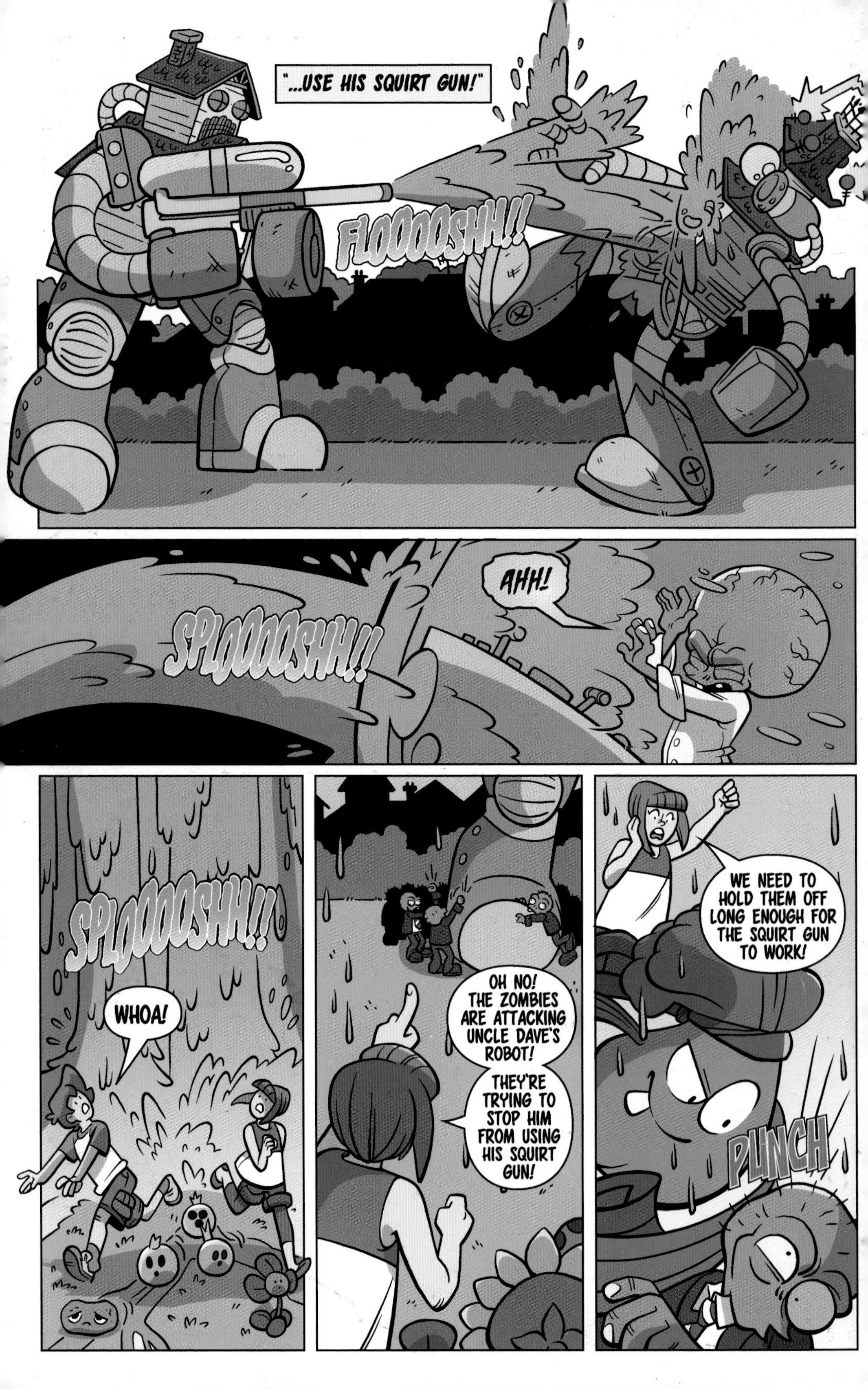
"...USE HIS SQUIRT GUN!"
FLOOOOSHH!!
SPLOOOOSHH!!
AHH!
SPLOOOOSHH!!
WHOA!
OH NO! THE ZOMBIES ARE ATTACKING UNCLE DAVE'S ROBOT!
THEY'RE TRYING TO STOP HIM FROM USING HIS SQUIRT GUN!
WE NEED TO HOLD THEM OFF LONG ENOUGH FOR THE SQUIRT GUN TO WORK!
PUNCH

HOLD TIGHT EVERYONE!
P-TOO
P-TOO
P-TOO
P-TOO
"WATCH OUT FOR THOSE GARGANTUARS!"
P-TOO
P-TOO
P-TOO
I NEED SOME HELP OVER HERE!
THERE'S TOO MANY ZOMBIES!
P-TOO
BRAINS?
PUNCH
CHOMP!
P-TOO
NATE?
NATE, WHERE ARE YOU?
SPANG!
P-TOO
P-TOO
MELON-PULTS! FIRE OVER THERE!
PEASHOOTERS! I NEED YOU TO TAKE THOSE BUCKETHEAD ZOMBIES DOWN NOW!
P-TOO
FWONG
FWONG
THIS ISN'T WORKING!
THERE ARE TOO MANY!
WE'RE LOSING!
NATE, WHERE ARE YOU?
PUNCH
PUNCH
"GRRAWRR-BEAR! COVER MY REAR!"

HERE!
FWONG
FWONG
PHTT
P-TOO
P-TOO
P-TOO
HORSE!
PHTT
GET ON!
LET'S TAKE THE FIGHT TO THE ZOMBIES!
KEEP THE ZOMBIES AWAY FROM THE HORSE!
WE JUST NEED TO HOLD OUT A LITTLE LONGER AND GIVE UNCLE DAVE AND HIS MONSTROUS SQUIRT GUN A CHANCE TO WORK!
THOOP
THOOP
P-TOO P-TOO
ROMP
ROMP
STOMP
FLAPPT!!!
BRAINS?
BRAINS.
CHOMP!
THE RUST! LOOK AT ALL THAT RUST!
CRAZY DAVE'S SQUIRT GUN ATTACK IS WORKING!
CREAK!
RUST
RUST
RUST

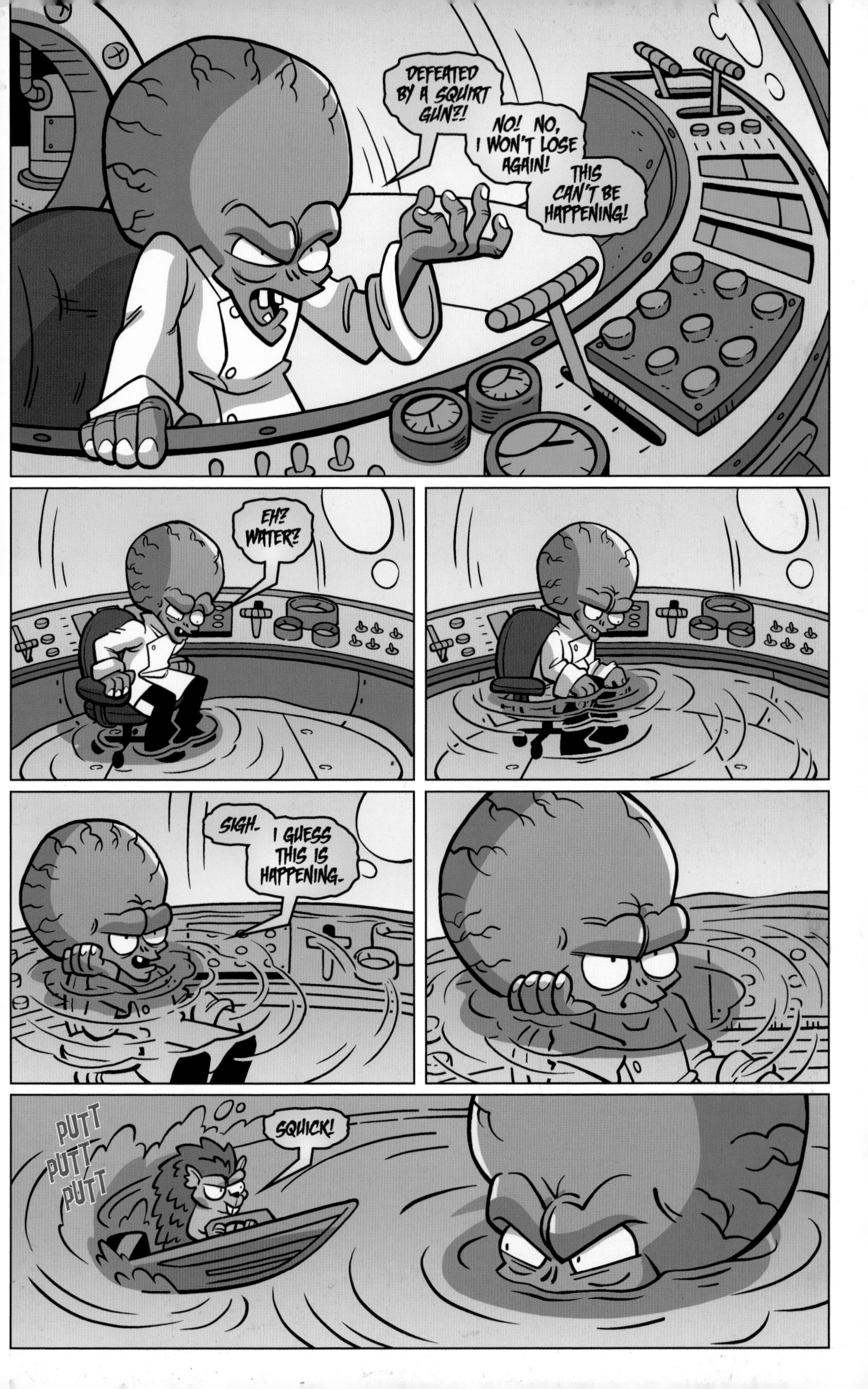
DEFEATED BY A SQUIRT GUN?!
NO! NO, I WON'T LOSE AGAIN!
THIS CAN'T BE HAPPENING!
EH? WATER?
SIGH.
I GUESS THIS IS HAPPENING.
PUTT PUTT PUTT
SQUICK!

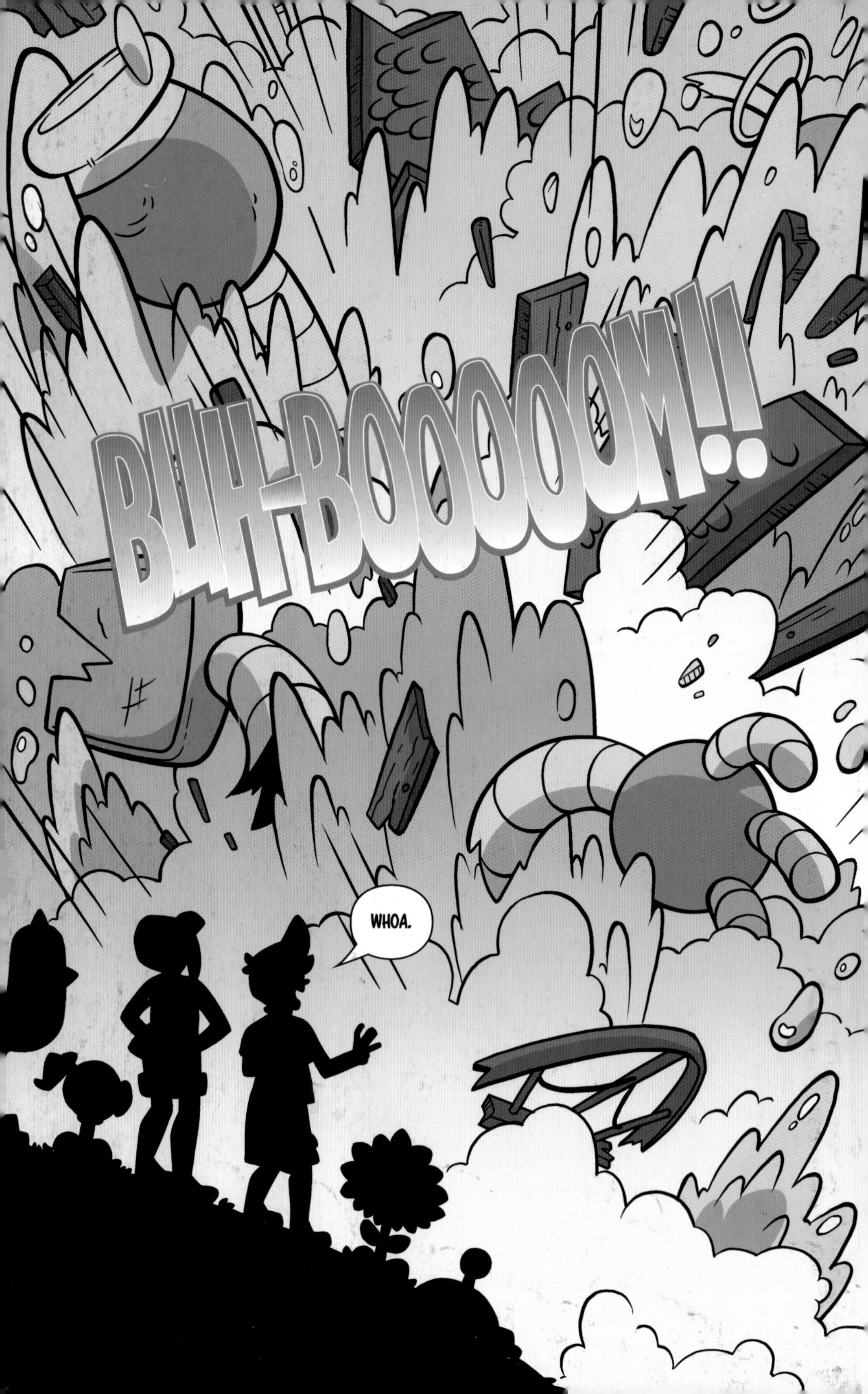
BUH-BOOOOOM!!
WHOA.

AND SO...
FEELS GOOD TO STOP THE ZOMBIES AGAIN, DOESN'T IT NATE?
IT SURE DOES!
BUT THERE'S NO WAY WE WOULD'VE WON WITHOUT...
...ALL THESE GUYS!
NOT ONLY DID THEY FIGHT OFF THE ZOMBIE HORDES, BUT THEY WERE THE ONES WHO FIGURED OUT THE GIANT ROBOT'S WEAKNESS TO WATER!

WHICH IS WHY I'M TREATING ALL OF THEM TO AN ALL-EXPENSE-PAID OVERNIGHT STAY...

...AT CRAZY DAVE'S GIANT ICE CREAM MACHINE HOUSE!

SOON, THE PARTY BEGINS!
TAP TAP TAP
EH? SOMEONE AT THE DOOR? MAYBE MORE PLANTS?

Open!
HELLO!
EH? ZOMBOSS?
LOOK DOWN.
HUH?
POUND
OWW! OWW! OUCHIE! OWW!
YOU'RE RIGHT, MR. STUBBINS.
EVEN THOUGH WE NEVER SEEM TO WIN ANY OF THE LARGER VICTORIES...
WHRR
WHRR
ZOOM
SQUICK!
...SOMETIMES IT'S THE LITTLE THINGS THAT COUNT.
THE END

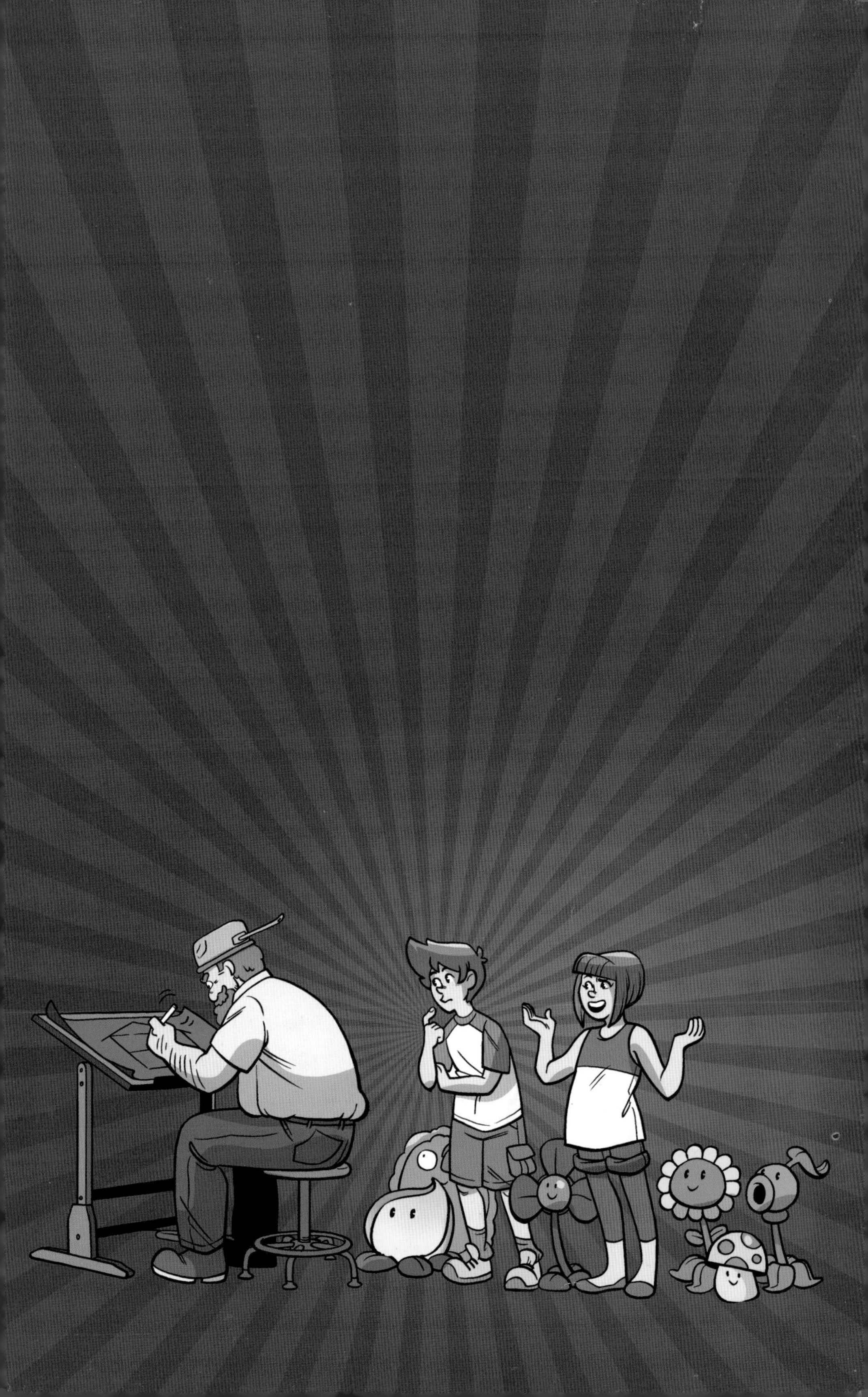

PLANTS VS. ZOMBIES: BETTER HOMES AND GUARDENS
COVER PENCILS BY CHRISTIANNE GILLENARDO-GOUDREAU

PLANTS VS. ZOMBIES: BETTER HOMES AND GUARDENS
COVER INKS BY CHRISTIANNE GILLENARDO-GOUDREAU

LINE ART FROM BETTER HOMES AND GUARDENS, PAGES 18–21, BY ARTIST CHRISTIANNE GILLENARDO-GOUDREAU!
WELCOME

NiGel

CREATOR BIOS

PAUL TOBIN enjoys that his author photo makes him look insane, and he once accidentally cut his ear with a potato chip. He doesn't know how it happened, either. Life is so full of mystery. If you ask him about the Potato Chip Incident, he'll just make up a story. That's what he does. He's written hundreds of stories for Marvel, DC, Dark Horse, and many others, including such creator-owned titles as *Colder* and *Bandette*, as well as *Prepare to Die!*—his debut novel. His *Genius Factor* series of novels about a fifth-grade genius and his war against the Red Death Tea Society debuted in March 2016 with *How to Capture an Invisible Cat*, from Bloomsbury Publishing, and continued in early 2017 with *How to Outsmart a Billion Robot Bees*. Paul has won some Very Important Awards for his writing but so far none for his karaoke skills.

Paul Tobin

CHRISTIANNE GILLENARDO-GOUDREAU is a comic artist and illustrator from Portland, Oregon. Her work has been featured in various anthologies and comics, including *Beyond: A Queer Sci-Fi And Fantasy Anthology*, *Plants vs. Zombies*, *Harrow County*, and *Dept. H*. She is currently the interior artist for the series *I am Hexed*, by Kirsten Thompson. She lives with her wife, Donna, and their dumb cats, Hot Dog and Pancake.

Christianne
Gillenardo-Goudreau

Heather Breckel

HEATHER BRECKEL went to the Columbus College of Art and Design for animation. She decided animation wasn't for her, so she switched to comics. She's been working as a colorist for nearly ten years and has worked for nearly every major comics publisher out there. When she's not burning the midnight oil in a deadline crunch, she's either dying a bunch in videogames or telling her cats to stop running around at two in the morning.

Steve Dutro

STEVE DUTRO is an Eisner Award-nominated comic-book letterer from Redding, California, who can also drive a tractor. He graduated from the Kubert School and has been lettering comics since the days when foil-embossed covers were cool, working for Dark Horse (*The Fifth Beatle*, *I Am a Hero*, *Planet of the Apes*, *Star Wars*), Viz, Marvel, and DC. He has submitted a request to the Department of Homeland Security that in the event of a zombie apocalypse he be put in charge of all digital freeway signs so citizens can be alerted to avoid nearby brain-eatings and the like. He finds the *Plants vs. Zombies* game to be a real stress-fest, but highly recommends the *Plants vs. Zombies* table on *Pinball FX2* for game-room hipsters.

ALSO AVAILABLE FROM DARK HORSE!

THE HIT VIDEO GAME CONTINUES ITS COMIC BOOK INVASION!

PLANTS VS. ZOMBIES: LAWNMAGEDDON
Crazy Dave—the babbling-yet-brilliant inventor and top-notch neighborhood defender—helps young adventurer Nate fend off a zombie invasion that threatens to overrun the peaceful town of Neighborville in *Plants vs. Zombies: Lawnmageddon*! Their only hope is a brave army of chomping, squashing, and pea-shooting plants! A wacky adventure for zombie zappers young and old!
ISBN 978-1-61655-192-6 | $9.99

THE ART OF PLANTS VS. ZOMBIES
Part zombie memoir, part celebration of zombie triumphs, and part anti-plant screed, *The Art of Plants vs. Zombies* is a treasure trove of never-before-seen concept art, character sketches, and surprises from PopCap's popular *Plants vs. Zombies* games!
ISBN 978-1-61655-331-9 | $9.99

PLANTS VS. ZOMBIES: TIMEPOCALYPSE
Crazy Dave helps Patrice and Nate Timely fend off Zomboss' latest attack in *Plants vs. Zombies: Timepocalypse*! This new standalone tale will tickle your funny bones and thrill your brains through any timeline!
ISBN 978-1-61655-621-1 | $9.99

PLANTS VS. ZOMBIES: BULLY FOR YOU
Patrice and Nate are ready to investigate a strange college campus to keep the streets safe from zombies!
ISBN 978-1-61655-889-5 | $9.99

PLANTS VS. ZOMBIES: GARDEN WARFARE VOLUME 1
Based on the hit video game, this comic tells the story leading up to the events in *Plants vs. Zombies: Garden Warfare 2*!
ISBN 978-1-61655-946-5 | $9.99

VOLUME 2
ISBN 978-1-50670-548-4 | $9.99

PLANTS VS. ZOMBIES: GROWN SWEET HOME
With newfound knowledge of humanity, Dr. Zomboss strikes at the heart of Neighborville . . . sparking a series of plant-versus-zombie brawls!
ISBN 978-1-61655-971-7 | $9.99

PLANTS VS. ZOMBIES: PETAL TO THE METAL
Crazy Dave takes on the tough *Don't Blink* video game—and challenges Dr. Zomboss to a race to determine the future of Neighborville!
ISBN 978-1-61655-999-1 | $9.99

PLANTS VS. ZOMBIES: BOOM BOOM MUSHROOM
The gang discover Zomboss' secret plan for swallowing the city of Neighborville whole! A rare mushroom must be found in order to save the humans aboveground!
ISBN 978-1-50670-037-3 | $9.99

PLANTS VS. ZOMBIES: BATTLE EXTRAVAGONZO
Zomboss is back, hoping to buy the same factory that Crazy Dave is eyeing! Will Crazy Dave and his intelligent plants beat Zomboss and his zombie army to the punch?
ISBN 978-1-50670-189-9 | $9.99

PLANTS VS. ZOMBIES: LAWN OF DOOM
With Zomboss filling everyone's yards with traps and special soldiers, will he and his zombie army turn Halloween into their zanier Lawn of Doom celebration?!
ISBN 978-1-50670-204-9 | $9.99

PLANTS VS. ZOMBIES: THE GREATEST SHOW UNEARTHED
Dr. Zomboss believes that all humans hold a secret desire to run away and join the circus, so he aims to use his "Big Z's Adequately Amazing Flytrap Circus" to lure Neighborville's citizens to their doom!
ISBN 978-1-50670-298-8 | $9.99

PLANTS VS. ZOMBIES: RUMBLE AT LAKE GUMBO
The battle for clean water begins! Nate, Patrice, and Crazy Dave spot trouble and grab all the Tangle Kelp and Party Crabs they can to quell another zombie attack!
ISBN 978-1-50670-497-5 | $9.99

PLANTS VS. ZOMBIES: WAR AND PEAS
When Dr. Zomboss and Crazy Dave find themselves members of the same book club, a literary war is inevitable! The position of leader of the book club opens up and Zomboss and Crazy Dave compete for the top spot in a scholarly scuffle for the ages!
ISBN 978-1-50670-677-1 | $9.99

PLANTS VS. ZOMBIES: DINO-MIGHT
Dr. Zomboss sets his sights on destroying the yards in town and rendering the plants homeless—and his plans include dogs, cats, rabbits, hammock sloths, and, somehow, dinosaurs . . . !
ISBN 978-1-50670-838-6 | $9.99

PLANTS VS. ZOMBIES: SNOW THANKS
Dr. Zomboss invents a Cold Crystal capable of freezing Neighborville, burying the town in snow and ice! It's up to the humans and the fieriest plants to save Neighborville—with the help of pirates!
ISBN 978-1-50670-839-3 | $9.99

PLANTS VS. ZOMBIES: A LITTLE PROBLEM
Will an invasion of teeny-tiny miniature zombies mean the party for Crazy Dave's two-hundred-year-old pants gets canceled?
ISBN 978-1-50670-840-9 | $9.99

PLANTS VS. ZOMBIES: BETTER HOMES AND GUARDENS
Nate and Patrice try thwarting zombie attacks by putting defending "Guardens" plants *inside* homes as well as in yards! But as soon as Dr. Zomboss finds out, he's determined to circumvent this plan with an epically evil one of his own . . .
ISBN 978-1-50671-305-2 | $9.99

AVAILABLE AT YOUR LOCAL COMICS SHOP OR BOOKSTORE To find a comics shop in your area, visit comicshoplocator.com. For more information or to order direct visit **DarkHorse.com**

PLANTS VS. ZOMBIES: THE GARDEN PATH—
DETERMINE YOUR FATE IN THIS ADVENTURE WITH MULTIPLE ENDINGS!

Is it a brain buffet for the zombies or an *unbeleafable* plant victory? It's up to you, as you get to make the choices in this new *Plants vs. Zombies* adventure with multiple endings! Our story begins with Dr. Zomboss' latest plan of evil genius—*disguising* his zombies as each other, in an effort to confuse plants and plant pals Crazy Dave, Nate, and Patrice. Can the friendly fronds get past these dastardly disguises before the zombies sneak into Neighborville tourist attractions—and even Watson Elementary school—to unleash their hungry ways? Every major decision along the path will be made by you and determine if our horiticultural heroes end up facing their unfortunate demise . . . or victory! Eisner Award-winning writer Paul Tobin (*Bandette*, *Genius Factor*) collaborates with artist Kieron Dwyer (*Captain America*, *The Avengers*) for a brand-new, interactive *Plants vs. Zombies* journey!

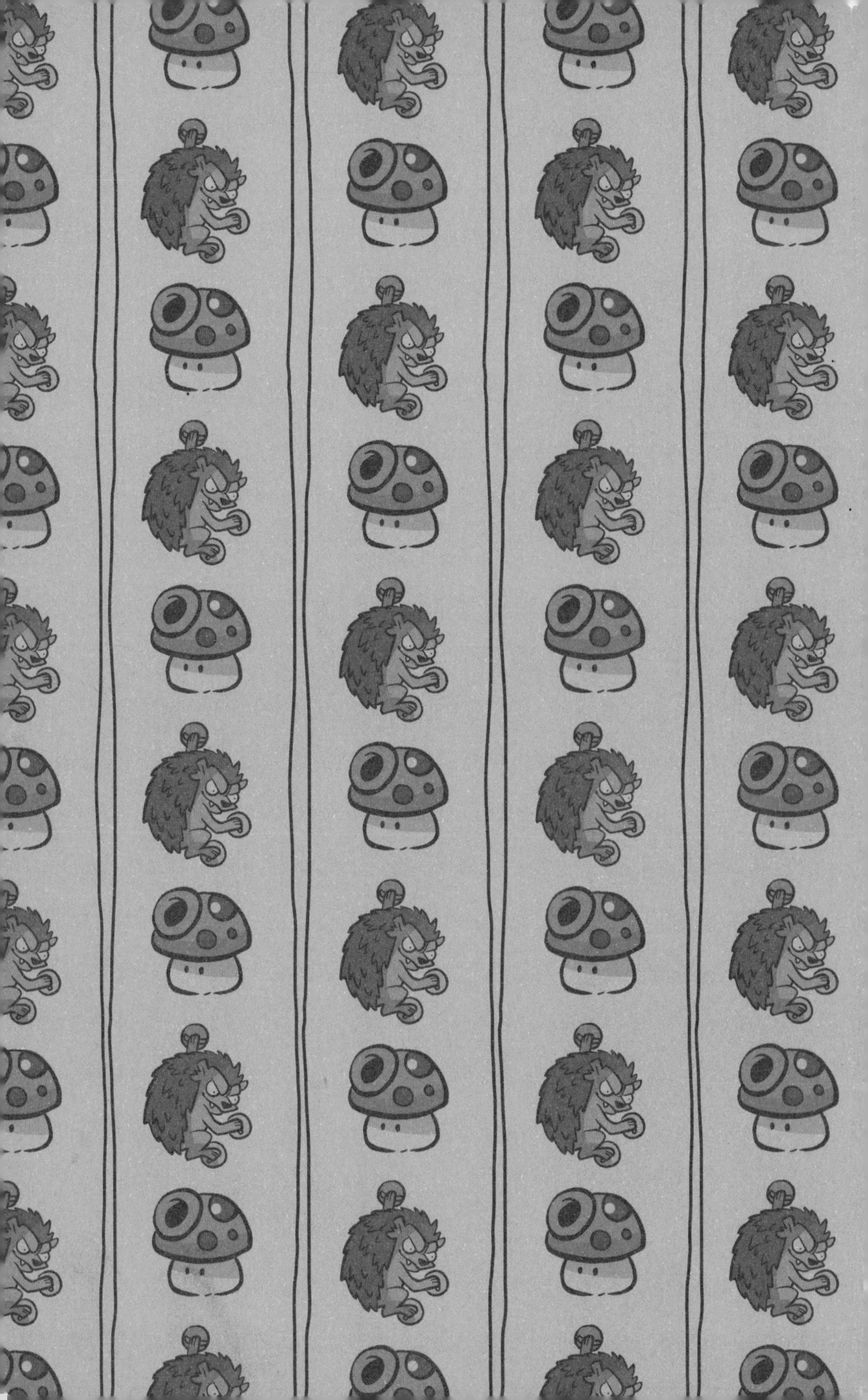